JULIA CAMMACK

Bella Book 2

Winner Takes All

Contents

Prologue

Her granddaughter had gone to make her a cup of tea. She lay back against the pillows and shut her eyes. It seemed as if it was only yesterday that all these things had taken place. How strange it was to remember them all so clearly after all these years. Perhaps she had been wrong, and God did judge you, punished you for your past actions. These memories had been pushed deep into the recesses of her mind, yet here they were. Perhaps, because her time was drawing near, those who had gone before were gathering. Some she would be glad to see, some she feared.

* * *

I

Part One

A Fellow Traveler.

One

Chapter 1 A Dining Car.

Finally, after changing trains several times, Isabella was on the way back to Paris. This train had a sleeping car, even private compartments, but they were expensive. She had been trying to sleep on the different trains' seats as she traveled, but it wasn't very successful. There was a dining car available. She didn't feel very much like eating but knew that her body needed nourishment. Eating something was the smart thing to do.

Entering the dining car, she chose a small table. Admiring eyes were cast in her direction, but she never noticed. She ordered a glass of white wine and a bowl of soup. Bella nibbled on a slice of bread and sipped her wine. Her thoughts were of Yvette. Soon she would be holding her child once more. That was the only thing that mattered. She tried to push aside all thoughts of what had happened with Serge. Isabella was not aware of the tall blond gentleman with an eye patch over his left eye. He, however, was very aware of her.

The soup was tasteless. After pushing the few vegetables that floated around in it with her spoon, Bella had taken a bit or two. Realizing that anymore and she might embarrass herself and lose it, Isabella called for the bill. She rose from the table, suddenly the whole car began to spin. She put out her hand to stop it, but it spun faster and faster. Down and down, she went until the blackness embraced her.

Chapter 2 The Perfect Gentleman.

Isabella slowly struggled up from the abyss. It was so peaceful there, no guilt, no regret. Bella was tired of thinking and feeling. Someone was speaking to her. For a second, she thought it was Serge, but it couldn't be. Serge was dead. The tears came unbidden. She tried to stop them, but they had been waiting there patiently. Now the dam had broken. They flowed unchecked with no end in sight.

Bella finally stopped crying and drifted off to sleep. She slept without any of the terrible nightmares that had troubled her on her trip from Metz. The smell of fresh bread and coffee woke her. She realized that she was lying in a bed. A real bed. "Where was she? How had she come to be here?" Isabella tried to sit up. The room spun, then settled down. She was not wearing her jacket or her shoes. Looking around for them, it occurred to her that this was a private compartment. Just then, the door to the other room opened, and a man stepped in.

"Good morning. Are you feeling better? I took the liberty of ordering breakfast. You didn't eat much last night. I also checked to see if anyone was traveling with you. You need not worry, I assure you. You are perfectly safe. My name is Joseph, but my friends call me Joe. I do hope that we can be friends." He spoke English with an American accent.

"How did I get here? The last thing I remember, I was paying my bill in the dining car. I am so very embarrassed by my behavior."

"Please, there is no need to be. You seem to have suffered a great loss. Perhaps that was the first time you faced it. Now you have had a good sleep, please, have breakfast while it is hot."

She tried to protest but soon found herself feasting on a hot roll and drinking real coffee. For the first time in a long time, someone was taking care of her instead of the other way around. His compartment had a bathroom where she washed her face and fixed her hair. He explained that he had paid her bill, then carried her to his compartment with the aid of the conductor, who was relieved to be rid of the responsibly for an unconscious passenger, especially a lady. Her luggage had been retrieved and brought to his compartment. He told her she was more than welcome to share it with him. He had made up the other bed last night and would do so again. He jokingly promised to be the perfect gentleman, Bella would be absolutely safe. For some strange reason, Isabella believed him.

Three

Chapter 3 A Band of Angels.

Joseph, or Joe, as Bella called him, was tall and blond with a bad scar that ran from his hairline to his ear. He wore a patch over that eye. "I tried to dodge a bayonet. It didn't work, so now I have the rakish look of a pirate," he told her, laughing. He had been visiting in the northern part of France to check on a group of nuns and to thank them. During the war, they had risked their lives by caring for him.

He explained that his plane had been shot down over France. He had managed to crash land it into a group of trees. The aircraft was on fire. It would explode at any minute. Hurriedly, he climbed out of the cockpit and, seconds before it became a fiery ball, dropped the rest of the way. Hitting the ground, he twisted his ankle.

Suddenly a German soldier appeared out of nowhere. Joe tried to stand, but the stabbing pain in his ankle caused him to twist and fall. The bayonet that had been aimed at his heart caught him in the face. The man drew back the rifle to stab him again, but by then, Joe's gun was in his hand. He fired. The soldier's body crumpled to the ground. He hoped the man was dead and not just wounded. The only reason he was able to shoot him in the first place was because the soldier was almost on top of him.

The blood that was pouring down his face had blinded him. He didn't realize that one of his eyes was no longer in the socket. Shock and the loss of blood were taking over. He put both hands up to his face, trying to stanch the flow. That did not seem to be working well. He fought to stay conscious. It was becoming a losing battle. Out of the darkness came a band of angels. What else could it be? He felt himself being rolled over, then lifted. The trip to heaven was rather rough. He wondered why, then he passed out.

He drifted in and out of consciousness for several days. When he would cry out, someone would ply him with a strong liqueur to dull the pain. Strange visions came and went. Faces with white wings floated into view, then disappeared. Something limited him from turning his head. Pain seemed to be centering itself in one side of his face. Trying to make any sense of it all made his head hurt worse, so he stopped. He became aware of soft voices and bells. Yes, there were definitely bells. He drifted off once more.

He woke up to female voices speaking softly in French. He had taken French in school, but that was so long ago. If he was not mistaken, there was some Latin. How strange. He tried to raise his head. The pain shot through him with such force, he cried out. At once, a voice silenced him. He realized there was more than one person in the room. It must be night, the room was dark. Why didn't they put on a light?

"Please, you hurt. No move, yes? This home for woman..Sisters. Mother be here for look you. I give for pain."

A spoon full of a fiery liquid was slipped into his mouth, and he felt it heat his body. It was followed by two or three more. It did seem to dull the pain. He tried to thank her, but the effort to move his lips hurt him. The liqueur was working. Once more, he slept.

Joe did not know how long he had been asleep, but the bells were ringing when he woke. He thought back to the earlier conversation. Now things made sense. This was a convent. How he had come to be here was a mystery. There didn't seem to be anyone in the room. Gingerly he put his hands up to feel his face. There were thick and balky bandages covering it and his head. No wonder he thought it was dark. The pain, when he tried to move his head, had a beat that was regulated by his pulse. His ankle hurt.

At that moment, the door opened, and several people entered. A woman spoke softly, then touched his shoulder. He reached his hand up to clasp hers. She patted him, then gave some instructions in French.

" Mother say rest, no to move. You want food? Soup. Yes? " He recognized the voice. It was the woman from earlier. He had so many questions, but his mouth did not want to work. Joe tried to nod his head, but that did not work either. It just sent waves of pain crashing over him.

"I be novitiate. One year, I be nun. You safe here. German man, no here. Is gone. You eat. You sleep. Make better."

Four

Chapter 4 Returned from the Dead.

J oe had no idea how long he had been there. The Sisters had taken care of him at grave risk to themselves. Slowly, one day at a time, he healed. It was hard to get used to seeing with only one eye. It threw his depth perception off, and the scare pulled at the side of his face. The nuns had heard the plane crash along with the explosion and then the gunfire. Had they not found him when they did, he would have bled to death.

They had carried him back to the convent. Both military uniforms had been burned in the stove. The German's body had joined others in the tiny church cemetery. It was a remote place, and for the most part, the enemy ignored them and left them in peace. Just to be sure, Joe's bed had been placed in a storeroom behind a pile of old furniture. Someone would need to look extremely close to discover him.

The plane had crash and burned far from the convent. Hopefully, if someone found it, there would be no way of knowing that the pilot had survived. That was his prayer. His presence would be a death sentence for his saviors.

Several months later, after the country had been liberated, Joe was taken to a military field hospital. A surgeon checked him out and was amazed at the care he had received. They had sent him back to headquarters. After receiving a medal, he felt he did not deserve, he was discharged. His family, in America had thought him dead. After his safe return, they assumed he would take up his position at the firm. They also believed he would marry the young woman he was engaged to before the war. Neither of these things happened.

Five

Chapter 5 Stories Shared.

The war had changed him. He was still charming, warm, and charismatic, but now there was a more sober side to him. Life had a different meaning. He wanted to make a change in the way the family company did business. Money and social standing were no longer important to him. The same could not be said for his fiancé. Prestige was essential to her. She was embarrassed by his appearance. His brother had taken over running the company in his absence and apparently, absconded with his fiancé as well.

Joseph had always handled the overseas accounts. He was more than happy to take on that responsibility again now that the war was over. He began carefully knitting the business back together, gathering new contacts in Europe. There was great satisfaction in seeing the world he had fought for becoming stable. Life before WW1 seemed shallow. He believed in the power of new beginnings.

Joe realized that his place in the company had changed. His father still owned the business, but his brother was firmly in charge, and was not about to abdicate. Joseph insisted the foreign accounts, should now belong to a separate company in which, he owned controlling interest. The family protested but soon concluded, that if they refused, Joseph could take his clients, work with some other firm, and cut them out completely. This new arrangement meant, the apartment in France, and the townhouse in London were his, and Joe alone would made all the decisions as to the direction the new firm would take.

Bella heard the sincerity in Joe's voice. The tone was light, but there was a depth there that shone through. She found herself telling him her story, leaving out only her true relationship with the German officer who had saved her daughter and herself. That part, she would take to her grave.

Soon they were talking and laughing like old friends. Terrible things had happened to them both. Not only had they miraculously survived, but their lives had taken a turn for the best. He told her of his plans for his company's future, how he intended to buy the other shares until he owned the business outright. She told him about her little girl waiting in England. How eager she was to get home to Yvette and to start a business again. They both had wonderful things to look forward to.

Bella realized that it had been a long time since she had been so relaxed around another human being. For some reason, she felt as if she could trust this man. How strange to meet someone on a train and feel as if you had known them all your life. When it came time to retire, Joe had the steward pull down the extra bed for himself and gave her privacy to change into her nightdress.

She thanked him again for taking such good care of her. He laughed and gave her an unexpected hug, telling her that it had been his pleasure. She was shocked at her reaction to his embrace. It had been a long time since a man had held her, that was what she told herself, but sleep did not come easy. When it did, there were only sweet dreams.

* * *

Six

Chapter 6 Dancing and Drizzle.

They arrived in Paris early the next morning. Joe took charge of finding a porter for their luggage and a taxi. He delivered her to a tiny hotel just around the corner from his apartment. There were business meetings that needed his attention. As he left, he asked her to dinner that evening. She was eager to leave for Calais, then on to England, but not keen on leaving Joseph. She would make arrangements for the train tomorrow, but tonight they would share a lovely dinner together. When she agreed, he grinned, reached down, lifted her chin, and kissed her. Bella stood staring at the door for several seconds after he shut it. "It was a short, quick kiss," she told herself. "Don't make more of it than that."

Bella had lunch in the restaurant next door, took a walk, then returned to her room. As was common in hotels, she had booked the bath down the hall where she had a long soak.

Returning to her room, Isabella took great pains with her hair, putting it up in the fancy style that she had observed the Parisian women wearing. Her dress might be plain, but she would not embarrass Joe by looking too dowdy.

There was a knock on the door. It was too early for Joe. She hesitated for a moment, and then someone knocked again. She opened the door, and the concierge, presented her with a small box. "This came for you, Mademoiselle." After he left, Bella opened it to find a corsage, a beautiful spray of tiny orchids, and a card that read," Until tonight. Joe"

Isabella had been ready for some time, looking in the mirror every few minutes to check her appearance or glancing at the clock that seemed never to change. At last, there was a knock. She opened it to find Joe standing there in a dark evening suit. He looked so handsome that her heart stopped for a moment, and she missed his greeting. He was smiling, saying something about how beautiful she looked. Joseph retrieved her wrap that had been lying across the bed and placed it on her shoulders. She picked up her purse and gloves. As if in a dream, she followed him out of the room and down the stairs.

They walked a few blocks to a lovely little restaurant, a well-kept secret known to a small group of patrons as one of Paris's best. The owner greeted Joe as a long-lost friend. He led them to a small table, then brought them a bottle of wine.

Isabella felt a prick of jealousy. How many others had Joe brought to this delightful place? She made herself behave, scolding her mind for even suggesting such a thing. No one could presume that a man like Joe would have been celibate. She was acting like a schoolgirl, not the mature woman she was.

The meal that followed was all that Joe had said it would be.

They ate, talked, and laughed as if they had known each other for years. There was a small band that played, so when they ran out of conversation, they danced. She couldn't believe it when closing time arrived. The band was putting away their instruments, and the wait staff was cleaning up around them when they walked out into the Parisian night. There was a slight drizzle that turned into a heavy rain as they reached the first corner.

" My place is just up the block. Come on before we drowned. "Joe was laughing," We hadn't planned on this." They arrived at a covered portico, where a doorman quickly opened the doors for them. Once inside, they shook off the rain to the best of their ability and entered the lift. When it stopped on the third floor, they stepped out into a small foyer. They stood there, dripping all over the floor, while Joe unlocked the door. A gentleman appeared from out of nowhere and was introduced as Andrew. Bella was upset with the puddles they were making on the black and white tile floor. Andrew assured her that it was not a problem. He brought them towels, and started a fire in the fireplace, while Joe pored them both a brandy. It warmed her insides, but her wet clothes were not much help. She had taken off her shoes and left them by the door. Now she stood in front of the fire, trying to warm herself and dry out.

"Bella," said Joe, " Will you please go into the spare bedroom and take off that wet dress? You will find a dressing gown there. It will be too big for you, but unless you do that, you will catch a cold. I will go upstairs and do the same. Andrew is here. You will be well chaperoned. He will make you a hot coffee or if you prefer, chocolate. I'll meet you back here."

She could have stayed where she was, but that did not seem like a wise thing to do. Taking off her clothes didn't seem too smart, either. She entered a bedroom with a small bathroom. It was tastefully appointed but very masculine. No woman's touch here. There was a soft terry towel robe hanging on the bathroom door. She peeled off her wet dress, towel-dried her hair, and snuggled into the robe. "Keep it together." she thought and hurried from the room.

Standing in front of the fire, she began pulling the hairpins out of her hair. Her beautiful Parisian updo had become a tangled mess. Coming back into the room and seeing her struggle with it, Joe had her sit on the floor by the couch. When Andrew brought the coffee, he found Joe carefully combing out her hair. Putting down the tray, he withdrew discretely.

The last time someone else had brushed or combed her hair was when her Mamma had been alive. She had forgotten how wonderful and how soothing that was. There was soft music playing, a lovely warm fire, and there had been the wine and brandy. Bella had spent such an exhilarating day. She did not remember Joe picking her up and carrying her to the guest bedroom. Laying her on the bed, he covered her with the quilt, kissed her forehead, and turned out the light.

Seven

Chapter 7 Shoes and Zippers.

The light taping on the bedroom door woke Bella. It opened, and a woman entered carrying a tray. Isabella, half asleep, wondered, how she came to be in this bed. She knew she was still in Joe's apartment, but the rest was a mystery.

" Good morning, my name is Susanne. Monsieur Joseph and Andrew have gone to the office. They will return in time for lunch. I have taken the liberty of sending your dress out to be pressed. I have brought you coffee and toast. If you would like something else, I will make it for you. Would you like me to draw you a bath?"

"Thank you, Susanne. Coffee and toast are fine." The maid put the tray on the bed and fluffed out the pillows behind her. "Was this a regular occurrence, finding a strange woman, asleep, in the apartment?" Isabella wanted to ask her this and a thousand other questions, but she couldn't. It wasn't her place to ask.

" I will take the bath, please, if there is time before the gentlemen come back." The doorbell rang, and the maid left to answer it, coming back with her dress. She hung it in the bathroom and began running the water. Bella finished the toast and coffee, thinking to herself how nice it was to be waited on and how unusual. The past days were a huge contrast to the last few weeks. She willed herself to enjoy it while she could. This may never happen again. Just go with it.

Isabella had dressed, brushed out her hair, and was ready when the men came back to the apartment. She blushed when Joe asked her how she had slept. It was disconcerting, having no memory of how she had come to be in a strange bed. Her poor shoes were in sad shape from the rain, but they were all she had. Joe suggested they go by the hotel to change them, before going to lunch. She was glad when they took a cab. Bella was sure the shoes would fall apart if she had to walk.

Passing through the hotel lobby, she felt as if everyone was looking at her and making wild guesses as to where she had spent the night. Holding her head high, Bella acted as if she did not care, but was glad to escape the prying eyes. Joe paid no attention to the raised eyebrows and to the fact that it was improper for a gentleman to accompany a single lady to her room. This was Paris.

Isabella realized there was nowhere for Joe to sit but on her bed. He laughed when she apologized. Had she not spent the night in his apartment? She needed to change her dress as well as her shoes. She retreated to the small bathroom. The zipper was stuck. No matter how hard she tried, it would not go down. Joe asked if everything was all right. She had no choice but to explain the problem.

"Let me have a look," Joe said, "Maybe I can fix it." She stood with her back to him, holding her hair up out of the way. His finger gently brushed her back as he reached for the zipper. She felt an electric shock travel down her back. "There." he said, "Cloth was caught in it." Then he kissed the back of her neck. Bella knew she was lost. She turned towards him. He kissed her gently at first, but his lips became more demanding. She began to moan softly as he slipped off her dress. His kisses moved from her lips, down her neck, and found her breasts. Soon all her clothes lay in a heap on the floor. He lifted her and carried her to the bed, all the while caressing her body. "Bella, my beautiful Bella. I have wanted to do this since the first time I saw you. I do not want to do something that will make you ashamed. If you want me to stop, I will" She arched her body to meet his caresses, reaching up to pull him closer. They stopped only long enough for Joe to remove his clothes. Soon he was inside her, moving with slow control that built until she exploded. He groaned in pleasure, following her with his own climax. They lay there until their breath became normal. He held her in his arms, whispering her name softly, gently caressing her. She lay there in a warm, happy, satiated state.

Joe suddenly stopped, "Damn, I will be late for my meeting. I am sorry, Bella, but we must skip lunch. I needed to talk to you later about your leaving for England." He began putting on his shirt and pants. Bella felt as if someone had poured ice water over her. Was that all he wanted? To get her into bed? Now he just wanted to get rid of her? She jumped up, grabbed up her clothes, and fled to the bathroom. She stood leaning against the sink for support. She had a cold hard knot in the pit of her stomach. How could she have been such a fool? She fought back angry tears.

Joe was knocking on the door. "Bella, are you alright? I must go now, but I will send Andrew to pick up your things. We will talk tonight. Bella darling… I love you."

"What? What had he said?" She opened the bathroom door, but he was already gone. She sat down hard on the bed. Had he said he loved her? Had he said that because it seemed the right thing to say, or had he meant it? How many times in her life had she had the rug pulled out from under her when she least expected it. Yes, she had come to depend on Joe, but never in her wildest dreams had she dared to entertain the idea that he loved her. " Don't count on that," she told herself, "Be careful. Remember, your child is all that matters. Yvette is all that is important."

Eight

Chapter 8 Joe's Apartment.

Bella dressed, packed her few belongings, and went down to pay her bill. The concierge informed her that it had been paid. He would send someone up to bring down her suitcase. He understood that a car would be coming to pick her up. He hoped her stay had been satisfactory.

That was where Andrew found her. She was standing in the lobby, purse in hand, trying hard to look nonchalant. He soon had Bella and the luggage in the car and delivered safely to Joe's apartment. He placed her things in the spare bedroom. After showing her to the kitchen, Andrew told her to help herself to anything she needed. Susan came only in the mornings, but please feel free to make herself something if she was hungry. He would return in an hour or two after picking Joe up at the office.

Isabelle had made herself a coffee and eaten an apple. She

wandered around the apartment, feeling like an interloper. There were photo's, probably family, a wall covered in books, a few she recognized, but there hadn't been time to read in the past years. The last time she remembered reading a book for pleasure was in Metz. How many lifetimes ago had that been? A parlor grand piano, open with a music score on the rack, a large desk, covered with what seemed like legal documents in neat piles, nothing ornate, but it spoke volumes. Joe had said that his family had a large business and social standing when he had spoken about the fiancé, who had preferred to marry his brother. Joe managed the family's overseas clients, but he wanted to live as far away from them as possible. He was his own man. That did not mean he didn't enjoy the things money could buy. His apartment showed that.

She came at last to Joe's bedroom. It was a large room with a bathroom off to the side. There were two chests of drawers, two navy leather chairs, an armoire, two bedside tables, and a large bed. It all rested on an antique oriental rug. There was a small fireplace, needing only a match to start the fire. French doors lead to a balcony with two wrought iron chairs and a table. From there, you had an amazing view of Paris. Bella heard the door opened, but before she could cross the room, Joe was there.

"Bella, I am so sorry I had to rush off, but this meeting was about a significant merger that I have been working for a long time. Suddenly it came to fruition. Did you find everything you needed? Oh my, Bella, I am so glad you came. Come, let me make you a drink, then we can decide what to do about supper. We have a lot to talk about." He took off his jacket and tie and threw it on a chair. Bella stood, looking at him, not sure what to say or do. Joe turned and saw the look on her face. "Oh, darling, forgive me. I am so out of practice. I just rush along with what I want. It has been a long time since I let myself care about anything but making deals. I just want to protect you, love you, but I will try to be patient and not push you. Could you learn to care…" Bella stopped him by kissing him. This time it was her mouth that became demanding. Food was forgotten. Now there was a different hunger. His bed was so close, so welcoming. There was no need for words.

Her hands fumbled with his belt while he tried to unfasten the tiny buttons on her blouse. Laughing, they gave up and removed their own clothes. He pushed her back across the bed. " Oh, my God, Bella. How beautiful you are." He kissed her lips and then her breasts. Bella urged him on. "Wait, chérie, we hurried last time. This time we will enjoy exploring each other. His hands moved down her body till he could cradle her buttocks. He took her breast into his mouth, running his tongue over her nipple. She whimpered with pleasure, pulling him closer. Now his hand had moved around to the inside of her thigh, his fingers seeking, finding. Bella rolled over, pulling him on top of her, wrapping her legs around his hips. They moved in harmony until they both reached the pinnacle. Spent, they lay there in each other's arms.

Joe pulled the covers over them, holding her close, nuzzling her neck, kissing her shoulders. Bella would have been content to stay like this forever. They lay there in a relaxed, warm euphoric state and soon fell asleep.

Nine

Chapter 9. Tea and Toast.

Joe smacked her backside, and rolled out of bed, laughing. "Come on lady. I'm hungry. I'll start the fire. Put on a robe while I see what is available in the kitchen." Bella watched him walk away. She marveled at his naked body. How beautiful he was. She had never had the chance to stare so openly at a nude man before. If he had turned and caught her looking, she would have been devastated, but he continued into the bathroom, returning with two dressing gowns.

Isabella could hear him in the kitchen singing off-key. She slid into the robe and went to see what he was cooking. He had found some eggs and was busily scrambling them. He handed her a toasting fork, a plate, butter, and a loaf of bread with instructions to go and toast slices at the bedroom fireplace. Soon he arrived carrying two full plates on a tray. Bella found the tea, honey, and some sweet biscuits. They sat there, happily devouring the food. The only thing that would make it any better would be if Yvette had been there.

It was as if Joe had read her mind. "Bella, it is time to talk about England. I must stay here for a day or two before this deal I am working on is finished. I am selfish enough to want you to stay here, but I know you are eager to see your daughter. Tomorrow I will send Andrew with you to Calais. You must be aware that there are many desperate and dangerous men about. I know you have bravely traveled all over France by yourself, but things are not safe. He will journey with you to England. I have a car there. He will drive you to your friend's home. Andrew is more than a gentleman's gentleman. He is a trusted confidant. He will see to your welfare and make sure that you are reunited with your child before returning to my London office."

She knew that he was right. She needed to go home. Wasn't that what she had been waiting for? Bella wanted to hold her child in her arms, but now she wanted to be with Joe too. Her love for Yvette won out. Her feelings for Joe were strong, but she had loved Yvette from the moment she had first held her. Reluctantly Isabella agreed. He was right. She would go home tomorrow. If tonight were all they had, they would make the best of it.

They made love again in Joseph's big, wonderful bed. Soon he was fast asleep, cuddled up to her back, his face buried in her hair. Bella lay there very still, not wanting to wake him. The tears trickled slowly down her face, dripping onto the pillow. How many times in her life had she found happiness only to lose it? If this should end after tonight, so be it. She would survive. Life would go on.

Ten

Chapter 10. Lady Maude's Advice.

True to his word, Joe sent Andrew with her to England. Having him with her, certainly made the trip easier. When they arrived in Dover, her case were placed in a small red roadster that had been waiting there. Soon they were on their way.

They pulled into the Moody's courtyard just as the children returned from school. Excited to see visitors and impressed with the car, they crowded around. It took Yvette a minute to realize one of the occupants was her mother. She threw herself into Bella's arms with a squeal of delight. How she had grown while Isabelle had been gone. Bella held her close, tears of happiness and regret for the time lost, slide down her cheeks.

Andrew was introduced to everyone. Soon, they were having a cup of tea and being brought up to date with the local news. Lady Maude seemed to understand that there would be time later for the story of Bella's search for Serge and what had happened in France. Andrew was offered a room for the night. He thanked them but, he was needed in London. There was an important matter that could not wait. He bid them goodbye, leaving Bella in Lady Maude's capable hands.

After Yvette was safely in her bed and fast asleep, the two women drew their chairs up to the fire. Bella told her of the trip from the beginning. She spoke of Serge's fate, the loss of his hand, his drinking, and then his death. She told of not only of Serge's passing but also that of Father Henry, her dear mentor. Isabelle explained how she had met Joseph, his kindness, his apartment in Paris, and his insisting on sending Andrew to see her safely home.

Maude watched Bella's face lit up when she talked about Joe. There seemed to be more to it than just gratitude for his help. The older woman had not been born yesterday. She gently questioned her about the legal papers she had signed to lay claim to Serge's property, arriving at last to the real relationship between Bella and Joe.

" I don't know." Bella was trying to be honest. She trusted Maude enough to tell her the truth. " He said that he loves me. Is that just something that he used to get me into bed? He seems genuine, but what if he just takes his pleasure where he finds it and then moves on? I don't think straight when I'm with him."

Lady Maude put her arm around Bella. " Sounds serious to me. If he didn't care, why would he send Andrew with you to make sure that you arrived here safely? Everything has happened extremely fast. You were extremely vulnerable, but perhaps so was he. Let us wait to see what his next move is. You have had a long day. Go to bed now. We are happy to have you home. Things may be clearer in the morning." She kissed Bella on the forehead, sending her upstairs with a "Sleep well."

Isabella set to work helping Lady Maude around the estate. There were gardens to prepare for fall planting and the house to air out before the cooler weather. Yvette was growing like a weed, so there were dresses to let down or new ones to make. It had been two weeks since she had seen Joe. If she kept busy, maybe she wouldn't think about whether or not he was back in England.

Her questions were answered the next day with the post. There was a small parcel with his return address, as well as a letter. There were sweets for Yvette, ginger snaps for Lady Maude, and a French lace handkerchief for Bella. His letter told her how much he missed her and asked if there was a way for her to come up to London for the weekend. He would send her a ticket and met her at the train. He would have come to see her before now, but his father had arrived unexpectedly. Isabella wondered if Joseph Sr. would still be there. She was not sure how she felt about meeting a member of Joe's family. They had sounded rather cold and judgmental. Hopefully, she was wrong.

Lady Maude encouraged her to go. It would be a reality check. Bella needed clarification when it came to the relationship. Yvette would be fine for the weekend. Isabella answered Joe in the next post. The ticket arrived several days later.

Chapter 11 Joseph Dean Sr. ..

Isabella arrived in London and was met by a smiling Joseph. He whisked her and her suitcase into the car. Soon they were motoring through the city at a speed that made her shut her eyes in fear. "You can open your eyes now, we are here." he said, laughing, "Not too bad for a one-eyed driver."

The townhouse door opened, and Andrew took her luggage. "I will put this upstairs for you, Miss Isabelle. Welcome."

As soon as they were alone, Joe swept her up and kissed her soundly. " Oh, Bella, how I have missed you. Why do you live so far away from me? We need to fix that as soon as possible. Only my father's arrival would stop me from coming to kidnap you and bringing you to London earlier."

She didn't know whether to laugh or cry. Joe missed her. He wanted her here. Her eyes filled with happy tears. Perhaps he really did love her. Did she dare to believe in happily ever after, or was it just a fairy tale?

Joe kissed her eyelids, her nose, her lips, whispering her name. " Bella, we need to dress for dinner. My father would like to meet you. He is leaving in the morning, so we have a command performance this evening. I would rather have you all to myself, but duty calls. Please don't be upset. I promise to make it up to you."

How could she be angry with him? Family was important. What if his father did not like her? What would happen then? She wouldn't think about that. How strange it must be, to have a parent who could pass judgment on the people you know. She took great pains with her appearance. Joe would not be ashamed to introduce her to his father.

The dinner was a slow walk over hot coals. Joseph Sr. was never rude. He was so very polite, it was painful. From the first handshake to the final goodnight, Isabelle was a bug to be dissected under a microscope. Nothing she could say or the questions that she answered helped. He took one look at her, or probably he held a preconceived opinion. She would

Eleven

Chapter 11.Joseph Dean Sr

Isabella arrived in London and was met by a smiling Joseph. He whisked her and her luggage into the car. Soon they were motoring through the city at a speed that made her shut her eyes in fear. "You can open your eyes now, we are here," he said laughing. "Not too bad for a one-eyed driver,"

The townhouse door opened, and Andrew took her suitcase. "I will put this upstairs for you, Miss Isabella, and welcome."

As soon as they were alone, Joseph swept her up and kissed her soundly. "Oh Bella, how I have missed you. Why do you live so far away from me? We need to fix that as soon as possible. Only my father's unexpected arrival stopped me from kidnapping you and bringing you to London earlier."

Bella didn't know whether to laugh or cry. Joe missed her. He wanted her here with him. Her eyes filled with happy tears. Perhaps he really did love her. Did she dare to believe in happily ever after, or was that just in fairy tales?

Joe kissed her eyelids, her nose, her lips, all the while whispering her name. "Bella we need to dress for dinner. My father would like to meet you. He is returning to America in the morning, so we have a command performance this evening. I would much rather have you all to myself, but duty calls. Please don't be upset. I promise I will make it up to you."

How could she be angry with him? Family was important, but what if his father didn't approve of her? What would happen then? She wouldn't think about that. How strange it must be to have a parent who could pass judgment on the people you like. Bella took great pains with her appearance, Joe would not be ashamed when introducing her to his father.

The dinner was a slow walk over burning coals. Joseph Sr. was never rude. He was so very polite it was painful. From the first handshake to the final goodnight, Isabella was a bug that was to be dissected under a microscope. Nothing that she could say or her answers to his questions met with his approval. He had taken one look at her, or he had held a preconceived opinion, that Bella would never be an ideal companion for his son. Without saying a word he had made that very clear. He was puzzled by Joe's attraction to her. She had no social standing, no formal education, and no money. As far as Joseph Sr. could tell Isabella had no redeeming qualities. His opinion was that she was a scheming little gold digger. He would inform his son of this at their farewell breakfast in the morning. Hopefully, Joe would listen and take his advice.

Joe did listen, then calmly informed his father that he was a grown man and capable of making his own decisions and choices. It would be great if his father approved, but if not, so be it. Isabella was someone that he had found to be brave, smart, dependable, and without guile. She never pretended to be anything other than who she was. That had not been his experience with other women he had known.

Joseph Sr.wanted to threaten him, offer to through him out of the company, or disown him, but Joe had been clever enough to sever all such ties earlier. He was completely independent of the family and the company. Their blessings would be welcome, but he didn't need them. What Joe wanted and needed was Bella. His father returned to America, leaving a clear understanding that he and his son would never see eye to eye concerning Isabella.

The weekend passed all too quickly. Joe and Bella didn't need anyone else. They were content to stay by the fire, their time spent talking, laughing, and making love. Andrew was the only one they allowed into their world when he would bring them groceries. They spent three glorious days in this cocoon, free from reality. Bella could not remember ever being so content. She knew that it would end, for the outside world was waiting, but for these few magic days, there was only this.

It was their last night together. She must leave in the morning. Cuddled in Joe's arms and half asleep, Bella's mind drifted aimlessly. Suddenly Joseph asked if she thought that Lady Maude would mind having him as an overnight guest? He would drive down in a week or two and meet her child. Suddenly Bella found it hard to breathe. Yvette was her beloved in one world, and Joe was her beloved in this one. For some unknown reason, she was afraid of what could happen if the two worlds collided.

" Bella, it is not just you that I need to be part of my life, Yvette must be a part of it too. I know that there could be no separating the two of you, so whatever the future holds, she must have a place in it. Her feelings must be considered, they matter."

Her heart felt too big for her chest, and Isabella was unable to speak. How could this be true? What was he saying? The future must be for the three of them?

Joe didn't know what to make of her silence. Was he mistaken in thinking that Bella loved him? Had he made a mess of things? He had been mistaken about a woman before. Had he done it again? " Bella, please say something."

"Joe. Oh, Joe, I do want you to meet my daughter. I just can't believe this could be real. Uh, Joe, I know she will fall in love with you just as I have."

That was all he needed to hear. Isabella loved him!

Twelve

Chapter 12. A Connecting Door.

Lady Maude had welcomed Joe warmly. He was Yvette's willing slave two seconds after they met. She flirted with him shamelessly, and he was delighted by it. Isabella's fears evaporated as she watched them. Time hung suspended in the bright afternoon sunshine. Everything in Bella's world, was perfect.

Joseph helped the men to pen up the sheep for the night, then washed up for supper. Jim came in from the fields, and soon, the two men were deep in conversation. An estate needed a great deal of care. James Moody explained all that went into keeping things running and solvent. His brother, Stephen would inherit the title and the properties. He was serving in Parliament since returning from the war, so someone must keep the home fires burning. They were still talking when Yvette came to fetch them and bring them to the table.

Yvette insisted that Joe read to her before bed instead of her mother but was asleep after the first page. Bella tucked the covers around her little girl, kissed her, and turned out the light. They walked arm in arm down the stairs to the drawing-room. The four of them played cards for a while, but morning would come early for Jim and Maude, so they soon bid them goodnight.

Lady Maude had discretely placed Joe in the bedroom next to Bella's, where there was a connecting door. Isabella felt extremely naughty as she slipped, nightdress clad, into the adjoining room, and into the big brass bed where Joe awaited her with open arms. Sleeping alone was beginning to feel strange.

Thirteen

Chapter 13. New Puppies and Fox Hunting.

Joe had slid out of bed and left Bella sleeping. He found his way downstairs, and soon he and Yvette were out in the paddock, inspecting the new puppies born during the night. Jim had said she could name them. That was where Isabella found them. They were in an earnest discussion about the merit of each pup and the most appropriate of kennel names. Once they were registered, they would have the pedigree name their new owner would give them. Some might go on to become champions, but for now, the puppies would stay on the estate.

Both Joe and her daughter were wearing bits of straw from sitting in the hay. They had taken their task very seriously and now, were introducing each of the three females and the four males to Bella as if it were the most important thing in the world. She thought of all the hard-corporate decisions Joseph had to make every day, yet, here he was, carefully considering puppy names with the same thoughtfulness. She bent over to kiss him. As she did, the smell of the new pups, hay, and manure made her stomach lurch.

She hadn't had anything to eat this morning, so she retreated to the house to help with making breakfast. By the time the others had returned and washed up, she was halfway through toast and scrambled eggs. They happily joined her.

The next day, there was to be a fox hunt. Lady Maude had been busy preparing for the hunters and their grooms, as well as the horses. Everyone had a job, even Yvette. Joseph was no exception. He pitched in gladly. By the time everyone was ready for bed, they were exhausted. For the first time since they had been together, Joe and Bella were content just to fall asleep in each other's arms.

The fox hunt was a big success. Jim's brother had come down from London to participate, along with some of his peers. Most of the Moody children had come home with their spouses and children. There were people everywhere. Lady Maude had hired extra help for the estate. It was not exactly the visit that Isabella had planned, but Joe had been fine with all of it. He watched this family with amazement. They laughed, fought, teased, but through it all, the house was filled with love. Jim's older brother, Stephen, who had become the Lord of the manor upon his father's death, was so considerate of the rest of his siblings and his mother. He told Joe how much he appreciated Jim and the challenging task of keeping everything going. He hoped someday to be able to make it up to him.

Joe could not deny the fact that he was envious. He could not remember a time when someone in his family had not been jockeying for the position of top dog. He stood back and observed this crazy, noisy group of people, knowing that they would defend each other against the world. He could not say that for his own family.

The following day was hectic. Everyone was preparing to leave. Joseph too, needed to get back to London. Yvette was inconsolable. She saw no reason for her champion to go. He told her she must stay to take care of the puppies till he came back. The puppies needed her. Bella too, put on a brave face but knew how much she would miss him.

Fourteen

Chapter 14 An Unexpected Situation.

The weeks seemed to drag by. Bella kept herself busy, trying not to think about when she would see Joe again. It did not help that Yvette asked every day when he would be coming back. She had snapped at her child. That was not like her. Lady Maude shook her head.

" Isabella, we need to talk about something. When was the last time you had your mens?"

Isabella looked at her in puzzlement, then the meaning of Maude's statement sunk in. She had not thought about it. How long had it been? She tried counting back, but the numbers did not want to stay in her head. She couldn't be, not now. She could not be pregnant. Even as she denied it, she knew it was true. What could she do? What about Joe? What would he think? How could she tell him?

Lady Maude sat her down. " Bella, you must discuss this with Joseph. It cannot wait. You have no choice. My personal opinion is that he will be delighted, but you will not know until you talk with him. There is no way to avoid it. This is not going away. The sooner you tell him, the better."

She knew Maude was right, but what would she say? His father had warned him. Joseph Dean Sr. had told him that she was out to trap him. Would this feel like a trap? Bella could not tell what hurt worse, her head or her heart. As if on cue, a letter came from Joe. He would be arriving on Friday and staying for the weekend. Now there was no choice. She would be forced to tell him.

Joe came prepared with gifts for his hostess, Lady Maude, and a large teddy bear for Yvette. He barely had time to hug Bella before Yvette dragged him off to see how much the puppies had grown. It gave Bella time to think over everything that she had been practicing all week. She had gone over it in her head again and again. There was no easy way to break the news that he was going to be a father. How would he take it? Maude had offered to break it to him. Isabella thanked her dear friend. This was something only she could do. No matter how hard it would be, Joe deserved to hear it from her.

Yvette had been sent off to gather eggs so that they could be alone. Joe could tell from the look on Bella's face that something was wrong. All the speeches she had carefully practiced vanished. "Joe," she said, "Joe, I need to tell you something. I'm pregnant. I'm so sorry." He stared at her. What had she said? "Pregnant? She was pregnant? They were going to have a baby?"

"Joe, please. Say something. " She had promised herself that she wouldn't, but now Bella began to cry. Joe too had tears running down his face, tears of joy. "Bella, a baby? We are having a baby? Are you sure? Oh, my God! We are having a baby!" He picked her up, spinning her around, then realizing what he was doing, put her down gently, as if she were made of glass. "Are you alright? Did I hurt you? Do you need anything? A baby! Oh, my God! We are going to have a baby! Does Maude know? Does Yvette know?"

"Joe, I am so sorry. I didn't mean for this to happen."

"I love you, you silly goose! I love your little girl, and now we are going to have a baby. I hope you are as happy about this as I am. I was planning to ask you to marry me. It will happen a bit sooner, that is all. Let's tell Yvette, and Lady Maude and the world. We are getting married! Oh, dear! …I am assuming…Isabella, will you marry me?"

Chapter 15. New Names.

Their wedding day was unlike anything Isabella could have imagined. Lady Maude had helped to arrange everything. The little chapel was filled with flowers, and there was a grand banquet prepared at the manor house. The Moody families came, all of them, as well as Andrew. Maude had altered her own wedding gowned for Bella to wear. Jim had the honor of giving the bride away. Yvette was carefully throwing rose petals from a little basket and looked like an angel in a pale blue dress. Joe informed his family of the matter in a wire. He saw no reason to invite them. It would have taken them too long to get to England in the first place, and he was sure they would not approve.

It was hard to tell who was the happiest, Joe or Isabella. Yvette, too, was beside herself with joy. Joe had asked her permission to marry her mother, and if she would be his little girl. Nothing could make her any happier, not even the puppy he had bought her from the farm litter. She had picked one of the smaller females and named her "Lady." Uncle Jim would help with the dog's training.

Isabella had a last name that was truly hers for the first time in her life. She was Mrs. Joseph, Daniel Dean. She had a legal last name, something she had never had. Not when she was taken in by her wonderful mother, not when she had claimed marriage to Serge, and never when she was a gypsy. If she had one when she was born, there was no record of it. Now, she could claim the name of Isabella Dean. It was right there on the marriage certificate. There would be none of the problems for her child that there had been for her, because Joe had adopted Yvette. Yvette too, had a new last name.

They traveled to the French Riviera for their honeymoon. They rented a lovely little house right on the beach at Juan-les-Pins. Days were spent visiting the sights, shops, and perfumeries, and nights in each other's arms. Too soon, it was time to return to England.

There was remodeling being done at the townhouse in London. Joe had purchased the one next to theirs, and the walls had been opened to create a much larger space. There would be a dining room, a playroom for the children, and two extra bedrooms. The small guest bedroom would be for a live-in helper. Isabella did not need a nanny but help around the house now that she was pregnant would be appreciated. She could not be there because of all the noise and dust, so she and Yvette stayed with Maude. It was the best they could do under the circumstances. It was such a minor thing compared to what they had already been through. Joe would supervise the work and hurry the men to finish sooner than later. He put a lot of miles on the little roadster running back and forth from London to Maude's. Bella worried about his frequent trips. He was not known for driving slowly. She would be happy to see all this come to an end for more reasons than one.

Sixteen

Chapter 16. Solicitors and Disinheritance.

The remodeling had been over for several weeks. They moved in and Yvette had chosen her own furnishings. The best of them, was a large dog bed for "Lady." There were just a few finishing touches to be made to the baby's room. Isabella was having trouble with the stairs. She was used to moving with ease, but her new shape was slowing her down. She felt like a beached whale. Joe told her every day how gorgeous she was and how happy she made him. He could not wait for the baby to be born. Business was going well, but he had farmed a lot of it out to Andrew.

There had been one curt letter from Joe's family concerning their marriage. To say they disproved would be an understatement. That did not bother Joe as much as it did, Isabella. She hated to think that she had been the cause of a rift between them. Joe shrugged it off, saying, 'It is their loss. We were estranged long before this. You and our children are all the family I need. Forget them." Several days later, Joe received a letter from the family's solicitor in London, informing him that he had been disinherited.

There were two things that Joe had insisted upon as soon as they were married. One was a visit to the American Embassy to have Isabella and Yvette declared American citizens by marriage and adoption. The other meeting was with his lawyers. He wanted an iron-clad agreement that would take care of Isabella, Yvette, and the baby if anything were to happen to him. He had purchased all the shares, so the business was his outright. He explained that Andrew was to be a partner in the firm, but Bella would have the controlling interest. She would own the house in London and the apartment in France. A small yearly stipend would go to the nuns in France who had saved his life. There were a few other small matters, but for the most part, everything would belong to Isabella. She would be a rich woman. Bella told him that this was not necessary. She was not interested in his money. Joe told her it was his place to provide and, even more importantly, to protect her and the children.

Seventeen

Chapter 17. The Accident.

Yvette and the pup had gone to visit Aunty Maude. The Moodys had become family. Uncle Jim was helping the little girl with the training of the dog. Joe and Isabella had the whole weekend to themselves. This could be their last outing before the baby came. They had decided to go down to Brighton and walk on the beach. Bella could dip her toes in the water even if she couldn't go swimming. They had a lovely day splashing in the waves, then drove down the coast to the White Horse Inn where they spent the night. They wandered the streets of the small coastal towns and had afternoon tea at a seaside cafe. It was almost dusk when they started back.

Joe was singing at the top of his lungs, and Bella was laughing at him for being so off-key. They came racing around a corner. There, in the middle of the road, was a farmer with a large hay cart. Joe slammed on the breaks and tried to steer the car to the side. There was the sound of metal ripping and horses screaming as the car tore into the cart. There was a terrible, searing pain. Bella cried out, then darkness overwhelmed her.

Chapter 18. The Dreaded Day.

Isabella could hear people talking, but it made no sense. She drifted in and out. Once, she thought it was Maude's voice she heard, but she could not be sure. Bella was in terrible pain. They gave her something, and she slid back into the void.

Someone was rubbing her legs, bending them, flexing them. The pain was excruciating. She begged them to stop, but the torture went on and on. How could they? Why wouldn't they leave her alone? She called out for Joe to make them stop. It was over at last, and they gave her a shot. Isabella drifted away.

Once again, they were dragging her out of her safe place. It was more than she could bear. All she wanted was to be free from pain. Lady Maude was there. Maude would make them stop. Instead, Maude was supervising the woman massaging her legs. Why would her friend be so cruel? Maude said, "We are keeping the circulation going. I know it hurts, but we must continue to do it."

What was she talking about? A nurse appeared. Suddenly she was screaming, not in pain but in fear. "Joe! Joe! Where was Joe?" She just kept screaming until they anesthetized her once more.

Isabelle knew someone was talking. Slowly a room full of people came in to view. Lady Moody was there. There was a nurse and a doctor, and another man she did not recognize. She tried to turn over, but that didn't work. She seemed to be encased in cement. Bella reached down. Something hard surrounding her from the rib cage to the pelvis. How strange!

She must have made a noise because they all turned to look at her. The nurse came to her side and began taking her pulse. The doctor shone a light in her eyes, then asked her how she was feeling. That seemed like a stupid question, but she could not think why. Maude looked as if she had been crying. "How strange," she thought, " Maude never does that."

" Oh, Bella, I was so afraid we had lost you too. You have been unconscious for weeks. We moved you to a private hospital. The care is better here."

"Better care? Why?" Isabella tried to put it all together. "You too? What did they mean, you too?" Suddenly she knew that the answer to these questions would change her life forever. She just wanted to retreat, retreat from knowing. Fear threatened to engulf her. She cried out, "Where is Joe? Oh, Maude! Where is my Joe?"

" Bella, there was a terrible accident, don't you remember? The automobile hit a farmer's cart. You were thrown free, thank God, or you would be dead too. As it is, you did nearly die. We have all been praying for your recovery. Oh, Bella I'm so sorry." Maude began to weep.

"What about Joe? Maude, where is Joe? Is he alright?" Lady Maude wiped her eyes. "Bella, Joe is gone. He died in the crash. There was nothing that anyone could do for him. He died on impact."

What was she saying? "Joe was gone? He was dead? No, no! She must be wrong! Joe couldn't be dead!" She grabbed Maude's hand. "Maude! You're wrong! Tell me you are wrong!"

"Oh, Bella, how I wish I was." Once more, tears filled Lady Maude's eyes. "We have dreaded this day, dreaded telling you. We couldn't be sure you would survive. It has been touch and go."

Bella stared at her in disbelief. Had she lost her mind? Why was she saying these things? The doctor stepped forward and took her wrist in his hand, "Mrs. Dean, try not to upset yourself. We are doing our best to help you heal."

Isabella wrenched her hand from his grasp. "Not to be upset?" She had just been told her beloved Joe was dead! How could she not be upset! Bella struggled to get up, but several pairs of hands pushed her back, and once again, there was a sharp prick of a needle.

Nineteen

Chapter 19. Loss and Lost Bodies.

Bella was trying to stay in the deep dark place. Something terrible was waiting for her, something she did not want to acknowledge. What had they told her? She fought against it, but the truth came flooding in. The physical pain was bad enough, but this was unbearable. "Joe was dead." That was what Maude had said. "She was lucky to be alive. Why? Why was she alive when Joe was dead?"

A nurse entered the room. "You are awake, Mrs. Dean. May I bring you something? How about a nice cup of tea?" How could anyone speak about such a mundane thing when all Bella wanted was the sweet release from pain that the needle brought. "I need something for pain," she said.

"I am sorry, but we are trying to limit the medicines. The doctor will be here soon." The nurse turned and left. Isabella was not sure which was worse, the physical pain or the one in her heart. Whichever one it was, she needed it to go away. She called out for the doctor.

When the doctor did come, he informed her there would be no more strong pain killers for her. He had been trying to ease her off them gradually. He was afraid she was becoming too dependent. "You are a young woman with your life ahead of you. It will not be easy, but you can do this."

"How could he say such a foolish thing? She had lost everything. There was no future." Suddenly, a horrid thought slammed into her brain. What about the baby? She reached down to feel her stomach. But it had a hard cover. She had felt this earlier. "My baby! What about the baby? Oh my God, What about the baby?"

"Mrs. Dean, we are so sorry. When you arrived here, you were in a cast because of the damage that you incurred. We have a full report from the other hospital. I am sorry to tell you, there was no way to save the little boy. Also, there is no chance of you ever bearing another child."

Bella could not comprehend anything the doctor was saying. It washed over her brain but would not stick. "No baby? How could that be? Of course, there was a baby. She was pregnant with Joe's baby." Maude would tell them. She wanted Maude.

Lady Moody had come and gone. She confirmed what the doctor had told Isabella. She had been thrown from the car and struck the ground with such force that there had been damaged not only to her but to the baby. Joe's body and Bella had been taken to a large hospital near London. There had been an emergency operation to save her life. They were unable to save the baby, and she could never have another.

No one at Maude's had known what had happened. Everyone began to worry when several days had passed with no word from them. Andrew had been the first one notified. He called Lady Moody with the grim news. When Maude arrived at the hospital, it was to find that Joe and the baby had died, and Bella was fighting for her life.

How could this be real? Isabella lay there, trying to make sense of it all. Who cared if there could be no more children. She had lost Joe. She had lost their baby. It would have been better if she had died too. There was no reason to go on. Bella just wanted to go to sleep and never wake up. Why wouldn't they give her something?

The strange man was back. He needed to speak with her. "Why? What else was there to be said?" He should go away and leave her alone.

" My name is Harold Brooks. I am one of the solicitors with the firm responsible for your husband's estate. We have taken care of everything on your behalf while you were unable to do so. Your husband was extremely clear on what he expected us to do in the event of his death."

Isabella wanted to scream at him. "Joe was dead." That was all she needed to know. Money and property were the last thing on her mind, but he just kept talking. Why wouldn't he be quiet? Why wouldn't he go away?

She had stopped listening. He rambled on and on. Suddenly, he said something that brought her back. What had he said? "Someone had taken the bodies? Who? How could someone do that? Who gave them permission?" She was shouting at him. "Why?"

"Mrs. Dean, you have been unable to communicate with anyone for many weeks. There was a chance that you might not survive. Someone needed to make decisions as to the dispossession of the bodies. Mr. Dean's father took charge of that. Through his English solicitors, he had ordered the bodies shipped back to America, to be buried in the family mausoleum. That seemed reasonable. The family's solicitor in London took care of the paperwork. A judge agreed."

Bella was stunned. Joe and the baby's bodies were gone? Would this nightmare ever end? What else could they do to her? There was no way of knowing where some of the people she had cared about were buried. How could Joe and her baby be on that list? There were no feelings, no tears, just a hard-cold lump where her heart should have been.

II

Part Two

Making a New Life

Twenty

Chapter 20. Yvette is Gone.

Isabella's cast had been removed. There was a large prominent scar running across her stomach from the accident. A nurse came daily to massage her and force her to move her legs to strengthen them. They would place her in a wheelchair and take her out to the garden for the fresh air. Lady Maude was making plans to move her back to the estate with a nurse. Bella complied with all this without arguing. The fight had gone out of her. If they had told her they were going to cut off her arm, she would have agreed. All she wanted was a pill for her pain, and to be left alone.

Lady Maude came to see her often. The last time she had been there, she had told Bella it was time to make plans for the future. "Isabella, you must begin thinking of what you and Yvette are going to do. You are not the only one who has suffered a great loss. Think of your little girl. She lost the only father she had ever known, a man she loved, as well as a baby brother. She nearly lost her mother. Bella, your daughter needs you more than ever now. You risked your life to save her in France. Listen to me, Yvette needs her mother! You are not the only one who has lost someone you loved. How many wives, mothers, sisters, and daughters lost love ones in the war? I, too, lost my husband, and a son and I almost lost Jim. We have no choice but to move on." Isabella knew logically that Maude was right, but it meant nothing. She could not make herself care.

Bella would be leaving the hospital in a week or two and moving to Lady Moody's. She sat in her wheelchair, staring out the window. The leaves were turning, but the beautiful red and gold leaves made no impression. Suddenly the door flew open, and Jim rushed into the room. " Bella, Yvette is gone. She has gone to London to find you. We have the police looking, but there is no sign of her. Help us, Bella we need you. Do you have any idea where she might go?"

Yvette was missing? How could she be missing? She was safe at Maude's. Bella shook her head. "What do you mean, she went to London? How? When?" Suddenly every nerve in her body was on high alert. "Jim, we must find her. Help me find Yvette!" She could not lose her daughter too. Jim carried her to the car, loaded the wheelchair, and set out for London.

Twenty-One

Chapter 21. Yvette's Plan.

I f you took the road to the village from Aunty Maude's, it was two miles, but it was just a short walk if you cut across the fields. Yvette had been planning this for over a week. The puppy would stay with his littermates in the stables. Leaving a note so no one would worry, she put food in her book bag and started out that morning as if she were going to school. When she arrived at the train station, the usual group of children waited to follow their teachers onto the train for a field trip. One more or less would not be noticed. She didn't have a ticket but planned to hide in the restroom when the conductor came around to collect. That part of her plan worked perfectly.

Upon arriving in London, she realized there was no one waiting for her. There had always been someone there to pick them up. Not only was there not a car or driver, if there had been one, she didn't know the address. She knew the house was across from a church. All she needed to do was find it. Bravely she shouldered her bag and set out.

Yvette had no idea how many churches there were in London. She would have asked for directions if only she could recall the name. It had a double bell tower and a statue of an angel in its garden. That was all she remembered. She trudged on and on, hoping the next church would be the right one.

She had stopped and eaten her sandwich and an apple at a small park. The sun had been shining when she had started out. Now the sky was gray. Big drops began to fall. Before she could find a place to shelter, the rain came pouring down. Her hair and her clothing were dripping wet. Her shoes squished when she walked. Yvette matched stoically on. A little rain would not deter her. She had come to London to find her mother, and she would not rest until she did.

The rain had stopped for a little while, but now it was getting dark. Yvette had been walking for hours. She was so tired. It was all she could do to put one foot in front of the other. How many more churches could there be?

She stumbled around the next corner, and there it was. Yvette had been on the verge of giving up. How could she have found it in a city as large as London? That seemed impossible, but there it was at last, with it's double bell tower and the angel. All she needed to do now was cross the street, ring the doorbell, and her mother would be there.

Yvette rang the bell again and again, but no one came. It began drizzling once more. Maybe her mother had gone out. She would be back soon. Yvette was cold, wet, and exhausted. She curled up on the steps, trying to shelter from the rain. That was where a passing policeman found her.

At first, he had thought it was a bundle of old clothing. A

very unusual thing in this neighborhood. He stepped up to see what it was. When Yvette saw him, she burst into tears. She was just a little girl, and it had been an extremely long day.

The policeman had hailed a cab and delivered her to the nearest police station. She was given hot chocolate and dried off to the best of their ability. Yvette gave them her name and information. It had taken a while to check on everything, but at last, they put two and two together. This must be the child that had been reported missing from the south of the country.

Phone calls were made. Lady Maude and her mother would be coming to get her. Yvette had accomplished what she had set out to do that morning. She had found her mother. Yvette closed her eyes and fell fast asleep.

When they arrived, they found her lying in an armchair in the captain's office, covered with a policeman's greatcoat. She looked like a sleeping cherub. Her hair had dried in a halo of rose gold ringlets around her face. Isabella would have a hard time forgiving herself for abandoning her child. She hugged her daughter so hard that Yvette woke up. "Momma, I knew you would come."

The ladies thanked the police for finding Yvette and taking care of her. Jim had carried her to the car, and they were soon on the way back to Maude's. Isabella could not bear the thought of stepping foot into the lovely home that Joe had provided for them in London. It would be too painful. Having returned to the living, there were things that she would need to deal with, but not now. For tonight, she would hold her child tight and be grateful for that.

They arrived at Maude's, and Yvette was soon fast asleep in her bed. Jim had unloaded the wheelchair and helped Bella to make herself comfortable in a downstairs bedroom. Lady

Maude made them a nice hot cup of tea, and Jim poured the three of them a brandy. Isabella had forgotten her pain in the mad dash to retrieve her child, but now she was hurting. Sleep did not come till the early morning. Even then, it was intermittent. She did finally doze off but woke up to find Yvette curled up beside her. Bella smiled for the first time in a long time and, pulling her daughter closer, fell back to sleep.

Twenty-Two

Chapter 22. Proving the Doctors Wrong.

M onths passed. Isabella had sold the beautiful home in London for a profit. Some of the furniture was sold, some was stored. Yvette and Bella had been staying with Maude. Jim had rigged up a bicycle to the bathtub, strapped her feet to the peddles, and helped her to make the wheels move. Slowly, her strength was coming back. Bella was determined. Soon she was able to make the pedals work by herself. Her legs would not hold her weight yet, but she was making amazing progress. Doctors had told Isabella that she would probably never walk again. She was intent on proving them wrong.

The physical pain was slowly losing its hold on her, but the pain in her heart was a constant companion. How unfair it was. Joe had only been a part of her world for such a short while. She had always been independent, then Joe had come into her life. For the first time, she found herself leaning on someone else. They filled that special need in each other. Now that was gone. All that was left was an empty aching space for Joe and the baby. She had no idea what her son had looked like, never had the chance to hold him. Bella loved her daughter. She would give her life for Yvette, but the loss of her baby and Joe, colored her every waking moment.

Bella stayed busy for most of the day. It was the nights that were the worst. She was helping Lady Maude with the estate. Maude's age was beginning to catch up with her. Some of the more physical things, were becoming difficult for her lately. Andrew had giving Bella an inside view of Joe's business and consulting with her on certain things pertaining to the firm's future. Isabella discovered that she had a good head for these things and enjoyed the work. Soon, she was going several days a week to London. Bella brought some of the papers home and discussed them with Maude. She fell into bed each night exhausted, hoping it would help her sleep. Sometimes it did.

Twenty-Three

Chapter 23. Going Home.

Summer was in full bloom. Jim's brother was home to help. There was so much work to do in the fields and the estate. He had brought his wife with him. Someday it would be her home. It was time for her to take over some of Lady Moody's duties. Maude was happy to relinquish a few, and soon they were working together, chattering and giggling like children. Lady Maude would tease her daughter-in law that there would be no double "M" for her. She would need to settle for 'Lady Helena Moody". Isabella could see that her friend was in good hands. Her help was no longer needed.

Bella had been able to walk a short distance with the aid of a cane for several weeks. It was not easy. Her legs would ache, and she was soon tired and needed the wheelchair, but it would get better. Yvette spoke English so much better than French. It was time for them to go home.

Andrew was going to Paris on business, and he would help them get settled. Isabella would open Joe's apartment. They would live in France for the summer. After that, they would see. Perhaps they would stay in Paris. Yvette should learn something of her heritage. It would be hard to leave Lady Maude. Bella had come to rely on her for advice and would miss her friend. Maude told her that she was always welcome, and that France wasn't that far away. Andrew went back and forth from London to Paris often. Bella and Yvette could too.

For the most part, the packing was easy. There were only a few things to ship. The apartment in France was completely furnished. They only had to take summer clothes and a few personal items. Lady would be going with them. Yvette could never leave her dog behind. Andrew would take the wheelchair to make it easier to travel, but Isabella was hoping that soon she wouldn't need it. Her legs were becoming stronger and stronger. It was time to make a new beginning for them both. Yvette wasn't sure about this. As far as she was concerned, there was nothing wrong with their old life.

* * *

Twenty-Four

Chapter 24. Exploring the Neighborhood.

I sabella took a deep breath, straightened her shoulders, and opened the door. The apartment was just as they had left it. Dust covers lay over the furniture, large, lumpy ghosts from a happier time. Somehow that made it easier. Andrew had offered to have the housekeeper come in and make everything ready for them. She had declined.

Bella set to work and with the help of her daughter, soon had the apartment tidy. Lady's bed had been unpacked. They put fresh linens on Yvette's bed, laid out towels and toiletries, and checked the kitchen for supplies. Joe's bedroom was the only space she could not bring herself to enter.

Yvette was fascinated by the parlor grand piano. Her mother promised she would find her a teacher. There was no point in having such a beautiful instrument and not making use of it.

Joe would have loved that. For a moment, her mind twisted, marking her loss once more. She forced it to return to the now. She would move forward in such a way as to honor his memory. Joe would not expect anything less from her.

Andrew had gone to purchase a few things, enough for their supper and breakfast in the morning. After being sure they were taken care of and laying out a plan for the next day, he bid them goodnight. They were both exhausted. Between the long journey and cleaning the apartment, bedtime would come early. Isabella fixed a little something to eat, then they both crawled into Yvette's bed and were soon asleep. Tomorrow, with Andrew's help, they would explore the neighborhood.

The next morning, Andrew brought in the wheelchair for Isabella's use. She wasn't strong enough to walk a long way without it. After breakfast, the three of them and the dog set out to become familiar with their surroundings. Isabella hadn't paid much attention to it when she had been here before. There was a lovely park for Lady, the school was several blocks away, and there was a small grocery store for everyday things. The chestnut trees had been late blooming this year. Their petals were beginning to fall and lay on the sidewalks like snow. They sat in the park to rest, and watched Lady try to catch the squirrels.

It had been a very full day. Bella was exhausted, her legs were aching even with the use of the wheelchair. It was time for them to go home. Once more, bedtime came early.

Chapter...25. Losing a Dear Friend.

Months had passed. Yvette's had her mother's ear for language. Soon, her French was flawless. She met several girls in the park while walking Lady and was soon looking forward to the school year. Isabella thought back to her school experience in Metz. What a difference. She wanted only good things for her daughter. They had found an excellent piano teacher and a voice coach. Yvette was becoming a very well-rounded young lady. How proud Joe would have been. How Bella missed him.

They had returned to England to visit with Lady Maude and her family. Isabella's dear friend had not been well. She still had her wonderful sense of humor but spent a lot of time just sitting by the fire. Her oldest son had left his seat in Parliament. Stephen and his wife were now living permanently at the estate. Maude had given up her upstairs bedroom and had moved into the small suite of rooms on the ground floor. The stairs had become more than she could handle. Isabella hated to see her this way. She had always been so full of energy. When they bid her goodbye, it was with heavy hearts. Bella feared that she might never see her dear friend again on this earth.

Several times, Isabella had traveled with Andrew to meet with clients in Luxembourg and Belgium. It was vital for her to familiarize herself with the business. These countries were making a gallant effort to recover from the devastation of war. She had visited the convent where Joe had convalesced after the plane crash. The nuns remembered Joe every day in their prayers, and now they would add Yvette and Isabella to that list. Bella had good days and bad ones when it came to prayer. There had been so many times when her's were not answered.

She had abandoned the wheelchair and been able to walk with a cane for some time. She would ache at night if she had overdone it, but for the most part, her progress was remarkable. Hopefully, the cane too would soon disappear. Isabella was looking forward to that. She would probably always walk with a slight limp, but that she could live with. There were much worse things than a limp. She could think of several.

Her dear friend, Lady Maude Moody, had passed away. There had been a well-attended funeral, with huge sprays of flowers everywhere. She had been laid to rest in the family plot. At least Bella had a grave to visit if she chose to. How many wonderful women she had been privileged to know. How she would miss Maude. "Remember," Sophia had said," Celebrate my life by living yours well." Lady Maude would have felt that way too.

She had made herself go into Joe's bedroom. For her, that was what it would always be, "Joe's bedroom." Strangely, she found comfort in being there. Curling up on the feather mattress to sleep, pulling the comforter around her, somehow made her feel closer to him. She had feared being there, but that was in the past. Now it was one of her favorite places. Soon she would ask Andrew to help remove Joe's clothing, but not yet. She was not ready yet. For now, this was enough.

Chapter 26. Bella's Boutique.

The years had passed. Yvette had grown into a beautiful young woman. She had graduated and was ready for something new. Bella had discovered a small store in Luxembourg that specialized in beautiful dresses in unusual fabrics. After several ladies had remarked how different they were and inquired as to where she purchased them, she contacted the owner. Would he be willing to supply her with a certain amount for resale? After several months of negotiations, they had made a deal that was advantageous to them both. Bella found a delightful space for rent in a high-end retail Parisian neighborhood.

Isabella soon had contracts with shoemakers, milliners, a jewelry designer as well as a Parisian seamstress that made beautiful lingerie. Her small boutique sold only exquisite, one-of-a-kind things. Soon, she established a second "Bella's" in

London. It seemed as if she had a Midas touch when it came to commerce. Yvette had a good head for figures and her mother's eye for fashion. She was able to handle the financial end of the business as well as finding unique and exotic items that appealed to the bolder clients. They made a great team. Isabella had the lawyers draw up an agreement that made them equal partners in the shops.

Over the years, since Joe's death, many men had sought Bella's company. She was beautiful, smart, and the fact that she was rich didn't hurt either. While Isabella had enjoyed their attention, none of them could compete with the memories of her beloved Joe.

Twenty-Seven

Chapter 27. Lucien Bousquet.

There was to be a wedding! Yvette had gone to purchase a car and met the young man who owned the dealership. She and Lucien Bousquet were soon inseparable. There was no need for a car in Paris, but they loved to explore the countryside. Sometimes it was Yvette who would drive to Luxembourg, to look at the newest in fabrics and dresses.

The last time she had been there, she had told Monsieur Yves of her upcoming nuptials. He had shown her two beautiful cream-colored pieces, one of Duchesse satin, and one of Venice lace. He would be honored if she would let him design and make her wedding dress. She had happily agreed. She would return in two weeks, for her first fitting. She could not wait to tell her mother and her fiancé Lucien.

Yvette and Lucien were planning to go to the City Hall for the Civil Ceremony, then two days later, there would be a church wedding. Yvette had asked her Uncle Jim to give her away, and he had happily agreed.

Jim and Andrew had become fast friends, and since Jim was no longer needed at the estate in England, he had been helping Andrew. They enjoyed each other's company and worked well together. Jim was surprised to find that he was good at customer relationships. He and Andrew discussed his coming into the business. He had a small inheritance from his father and was interested in using it to joining the firm that Joe had established. Bella was so busy with her boutiques that she was more than happy to welcome a third person that they trusted in a joint partnership. The two men were able to increase the client list experientially.

Lucien Bousquet had a large family, but Jim, Andrew, and her mother were the only family Yvette had. She had been to Nancy and visited her father's grave. It was just another grave as far as she was concerned. Joe was the only father she had known. It had been for too short a time, but she missed him. While she loved her uncle Jim, she wished with all her heart, that it could have been Joe walking her down the aisle.

Twenty-Eight

Chapter 28. Worst Things to Come.

Yvette had been back for several fittings. The dress was the most beautiful thing she had ever seen. Monsieur Yves had asked if her mother could accompany her on what was to be the final fitting. He had some business he wished to discuss. The dress fit Yvette perfectly. While she was changing, and the wedding dress was being carefully packed and placed in the car, Isabella prepared to meet with Monsieur Yves. Instead of going into his office as she had expected, he led her into the front parlor.

" I would like you to meet my wife, Ester." Isabella noticed that the woman had obviously been crying. " Her family is in the banking business in Germany. They thought that Ester had made a mistake, marrying a cloth merchant. They felt that she had married down. For many years, there has been very little correspondence with any of them. A month ago, we received a letter from her sisters. There have been several more since then. When they were girls in boarding school, they invented a secret written code to share things they did not want the grownups to know. There were things in these letters, things they were afraid to write openly. You have been a good friend, and now I must trust you to help us."

Isabella could see that the couple was deeply distressed. She immediately asked what it was they needed and how she could help. Ester explained that there were rumors, strong rumors about trouble brewing for Jews in Germany. People were becoming openly hostile towards them, and the government was making anti-Semitic threats. Something called the Anti-Jewish Nuremberg law has been passed, and there were hints of worst things to come. Luxemburg could not defend it's self against a German invasion.

"We are praying that this will soon pass, but we are concerned enough to consider what it is that we must do to prepare. Our dresses are shipped to you for your shops in France and England. With your permission, we will be making special shoulder pads for them. When you receive the dresses, remove the pads and open them. Inside, you will find monies and jewelry, things of value that must be kept safe. We have talked about this, and you are the only one we trust to take care of our property. Hopefully, we are being foolish, and all this will not be necessary. It is a huge imposition. We are embarrassed to ask this of you, but you are our only hope." Having delivered such a long speech, Monsieur Yves put his arm around his wife and waited. They stood looking at Isabella.

Bella sat stunned. There was no mistaking the fear in their eyes. "I pray that you are wrong, but I will do as you wish. Your things will be placed in a secure box in a bank in England for safekeeping. We must use a code word on the invoice when you start shipping these special dresses. This must remain between us and no one else." The Yves shed tears of gratitude. "Thank you, thank you. We will always be grateful."

The wedding dress had been loaded into the car, and they said their goodbyes. Yvette was so excited that she never noticed her mother's somber continence. Bella spent the drive back to Paris, praying that the Yves were wrong. The world was trying to forget the horrors of the war. People and the land were beginning to heal. It had taken a long time. Please, let them be wrong,

Twenty-Nine

Chapter 29. The Wedding and a Strange Request.

The wedding was well attended by every member of Lucien's family. Jim's brother Stephen and his wife had come over from England. It was a grand affair. Yvette, in her beautiful wedding dress, was the star of the show, as befitting all brides on their special day.

At the reception, Lucien's favorite uncle, the one he was named after, was very attentive to Bella. How she wished that Joe could have lived to see this day, but as the night wore on, she found herself laughing at Lucien's uncle's jokes and even dancing. It had been a long time since she had felt so free. He had kissed her hand when they at last bid adieu and asked if he could call on her the next time he was in Paris. All in all, it had been a perfect day.

Andrew, Jim, or Isabella traveled to England often on business. They had needed to stay in a hotel each time, so Bella purchased a Georgian era townhouse in London near Regents Park and had it remodeled. Joe's American fascination with plumbing had made an impression on her, so each of the three bedrooms had their own bathrooms. It made sense to have a place to stay when any of them needed to be in London for any reason. She retrieved Joe's furniture from storage and bought a few new pieces. Andrew and Jim furnish their bedroom. The third was for any guests they had. Not needing to pack and unpack made things easier. Having properties in both England and France had advantages.

Isabella had gone in London to check on the Boutique. There was a letter waiting for her. She was to call when she arrived and make an appointment to meet with a government official. Wondering what she had done, she made the call immediately. A secretary gave her an appointment for the next day. When asked, "In reference to what?" she could not provide Isabella with an answer.

Arriving for her meeting the next morning, Isabella was ushered into a private office. The gentleman offered her a cup of tea and invited her to sit. " You may not remember me, Mrs. Dean. I am the military officer that hired you to work as an interpreter for the armed forces at the end of the war. I have pulled your file, and we are up to date with everything you have accomplished since then. I am now working with the British Intelligence Service. You are wondering why I have invited you here. What I am about to share with you is top secret. We are aware of your connections in the past with the Resistance, and that you travel between countries with your business. You are in a unique position. We would be interested in recruit you." Isabella stared at him. What in the world did he mean, recruit her?

He continued, "I am sure you have questions. I will try to answer them to the best of my ability, but there will be things that I am not at liberty to divulge. You have an excellent reason to travel in France, Belgium, and Luxembourg and hold meetings in other parts of Europe. You hear things, conversations, innocent speculations, and rumors. We need you to take note of these things. Most of it will be just talk, but some will be important. There are things being put in place now that may be dangerous for the future of Europe. Would that be something that you would consider doing for the country?"

"I am not sure exactly what it is that you want me to do. Gather gossip and rumors? How will I know what is important and what is not? I am a French citizen by birth and an American by marriage. I have been warmly welcomed here in Britain. If there is something that I could do for you, I would be honored to do it, but I'm not sure I could be of any help." Isabella sipped her tea.

"That is true, but sometimes the simplest slip of the tongue or an innocent remark will give us information. You never know what will be of use. We do not want you to put yourself in danger, just listen and report back to us with anything out of the ordinary."

Isabella thought about the strange conversation she had had with the Yves. Was that the sort of thing he was speaking of? Without revealing everything, she told him about the cryptic letters received from Germany.

"Yes," he said, "We are aware of this newest development. Some disconcerting things are happening. The government appears to be leaning in a rather dangerous direction. Many of the things put in place in the Versailles treaty have been receded, and a man named Hitler, is becoming more and more powerful. Having said that, your information from civilians living in Germany is most definitely of interest. If you are willing to work with us, we would be most appreciative. This is, of course, completely off the record. This conversation never happened. He gave her his card, shook her hand, and asked her to consider his request. She agreed to let him know what she decided.

Chapter 30. A Baptism and a Surprise Confession.

Yvette and Lucien became the proud parents of a baby girl. She came into the world on their first anniversary. Much to Bella's delight, they had named her after Joe. Her name was Josephine. Isabella was a grandmother. She would be called by the English "Nanna" If there had been better news out of Germany, her world would have been complete.

The dresses had arrived from the Yves, and their secret contents were deposited safely in one of England's finest banks. She had taken a refresher course in German and had been working with the British government for some time. Most of the news that she passed on was of little use, but as her contact in the Home Office had said, people do not stop to think about what they are saying in front of a woman. Lately, some of it had become scary. She had been stopped by a policeman in Germany and questioned. Afterward, she was shaking so hard that she needed to sit on a bench until she calmed down. There were people in France who were spouting anti-Jewish rhetoric. German troops occupied the Rhineland, Germany, and Italy formed the Rome-Berlin Axis alliance, and now Spain was looking for trouble. *The whole world is insane. How could anyone be contemplating another war? What kind of danger awaited her granddaughter?*

There was to be a baptism for Josie. The preparations had taken Isabella's mind from Europe's troubles for a little while. All the Bousquet family gathered for the celebration, including Uncle Lucien, or Luce, as Bella called him. He had been to visit Paris many times over the past year, and Isabella had found his company refreshing. He made her laugh. She looked forward to spending time with him. Their friendship had grown. His wife had passed away several years before. It seemed strange that they could talk to each other about their spouses and how much they had missed them. They understood what it was to lose the one you loved. It drew them together. The family smiled and winked at each other behind their back.

That evening, after the day-long baptism celebration, Isabella and Luce had a late supper at one of Paris's bistros. They talked about how beautiful the baby was and how loudly she had registered her displeasure at the cold water being poured on her forehead. Later, the conversation turned to more serious things. Luce said, "The world situation is heating up. If there is another war, God forbid, you understand that both Lucien and I will volunteer or be conscripted into the army? Would you consider taking Yvette and the baby to England? I am so sorry to spoil what has been a wonderful day, but I have become very fond of you, and this has weighed heavily on my mind. I cannot imagine anything happening to you." He reached across the table and took her hand. She could see the tears in his eyes.

Until then, she had thought of him as a dear and trusted friend. The idea that he might be hurt or worse, killed because of a war made her realize how much she had come to care for Luce. What had begun as a friendship had slowly, over the months, deepened into love. While others had seen this happening, she had been completely oblivious. It had never occurred to her that they could be anything but friends.

Lucien stood up and came around the table. He knelt at her side. "Isabella Dean, I love you. I have been afraid of expressing my feelings, afraid of losing you as a friend. The threat of war has speeded everything up. If you do not feel the same, please do not let that end our friendship. I would miss you terribly."

That evening as Luce bid her goodnight, he kissed her on each cheek as had been his custom, but then he took her in his arms. The kiss they shared was anything but casual. It shook Isabella to her core. She hadn't felt anything like that since Joe's passing. She didn't want it to end. It was Lucien who pulled away. "Bella, I don't want this to be a casual thing. Perhaps I am an old soul, but this is too important to be taken lightly. I am willing to wait. You must think this over and be sure it is right for you. Take all the time you need. No matter what you decide, I will always be your friend.

Chapter 31. Chateau des Bois.

Except for a third cousin who rather fancied the handsome widower for herself, the Bousquet family was delighted to see that Isabella and Lucien had finally arrived at the consensus the family had known for some time. They loved each other! The majority opinion was, "About time."

Two problems stood in their way. For Isabella, it was her age. She was older than Luce. For Lucien, it was Bella's money. She was a rich woman. He was not poor by any standards but by comparison to her…

The family just laughed at them. No one suspected Lucien of being after Bella's money. As for the age thing, no one thought anything about an older man marrying a younger woman. It was about time that the table was turned, besides, if anything, Isabella had grown more beautiful with each passing year. They did tease Luce about becoming a grandfather to his nephew's child when they married. Lucien and Isabella had not discussed marriage. The fact that they were in love was new. They should be allowed to become comfortable with that.

Lucien took Bella to visit his family home near Epernay. It was a small chateau built over a hundred years before. It stood in the middle of a parkland. Luce had modernized the wing damaged by the last war. That was where he lived. The rest of the building had been preserved but never updated, Lucien apologized. It was expensive enough just to keep it from deteriorating. As Isabella walked through the ballroom, the library, and the sitting rooms, she could imagine what it must have looked like. You could feel the grandeur that had been Chateau des Bois. The beautiful old parquet floors needed to be refinished. The chandeliers had been bagged, the mirrors were crazed, and all the paintings but one had been placed in storage. Luce had hung the portrait of his mother in his bedroom.

The stable and carriage house had been made into a home for a farmer and his family. They took care of the property. It was their cows that munched contentedly on the grasses around the chateau. Rows of grapevines marched in neat lines into the distance. When ripe, the fruit would be removed and taken to the large caves to be processed and turned into champagne. That would be the three busiest weeks of the year. Extra helpers would be hired to help with the hard work.

It was strange, but Isabella felt as if she had come home. If she and Luce married, this is where they would live. Luce was amazed at Bella's obvious delight. He had been reluctant to show it to her. He had seen the residence she owned in Paris. There was no comparison between the two. Her apartment was so modern and chic. The chateau was old and dilapidated. It did have something that her apartment did not, secret passageways. When Lucien was a child, he loved to hide, and then jump out, scaring the new maids. He had received many a lecture from his mother, but it hadn't stopped him. Bella laughed with delight and could not wait for her granddaughter to be old enough to share in the fun.

Lucien had given Isabella his bedroom while he would sleep on the couch. That evening, while he was busy speaking with the farmer, she had changed into a beautiful negligee and poured two glasses of champagne. When he returned, it was to find Bella waiting for him in a candlelit room. Her kiss told him everything. Lucien picked her up and carried her to his bed. They spent the rest of the night exploring each other's bodies. Bella had assumed that after Joe's death, sex was a thing of the past. Luce soon changed her mind. He awakened a hunger in her that she had denied for a long time. When at last, they fell asleep, it was in each other's arms. Luce teased her that she had agreed to marry him because of Chateau des Bois. She told him it was for the lovemaking.

Thirty-Two

Chapter 32. More Than Just Gossip.

The next time Luce visited Paris, they went to the city hall and received a marriage license. There would be a small ceremony with as little pomp and circumstance as possible. The family was not about to let that happen. Luce said, laughing, "The Bousquet family would never let an opportunity pass to throw a party." Isabella had a different view. "Perhaps, if there were to be a war, it would be the last time the whole family could gather to celebrate."

Luce went home to supervise repairs to the antediluvian grape press. Everything must be clean and waiting when the grapes are ready to harvest. Isabella was in London looking after business. She also needed to notify Captain Stewart of her upcoming nuptials. Luce knew nothing about her work with the government. Bella hated to keep a secret from him but was not sure she should or could say anything. She had been told never to discuss what she had been doing.

It had been easy when she was single, but now the marriage would complicate everything. She had been doing a little more than just collecting gossip. There were people in Britain under suspicion of being German agents, but some in Europe were working for British intelligence. Bella was only slightly involved. She had carried documents back to England, among other things, but feared it might become more dangerous if some of the terrible rumors she was hearing, became true.

Arriving at the office of Captain Stewart, she was surprised to see several other officers in the room. After being introduced to them and being served the obligatory cup of tea, she informed them of the upcoming change to her marital status. They congratulated her, but they also made it clear that she could not share what she was doing with anyone, not even Lucien. If that were going to be a problem, they would understand. It did make their next proposition a bit more complicated, however. She could speak French, English, and German. She was a familiar face at frontiers and had been traveling back and forth between countries for years. MI6 needed her help. Isabella would be an ideal person to work with counterintelligence in Europe.

"Let me be sure I understand what you are asking. You would like me to become more than just a gossip collector. If I did, I could not tell my husband what I am doing?" She stood up." This is something I must think over carefully before making such a serious commitment." She left the office with mixed emotions. To do what they were asking would help if there was a war. Not to tell Lucien was the one thing stopping her from saying yes.

Thirty-Three

Chapter 33. A Panicked Call.

Lucien and Isabella were married on the first day of June 1937. The family threw the biggest party ever. Everyone had been invited to the celebration. Bella shook her head. "So much for an unintrusive, quiet ceremony." Yvette was her matron of honor, and Jose, toddled up the aisle on her pudge little legs, happily scattering rose petals and then trying to pick them all up again. For those few hours, Bella's world was perfect.

The townhouse that belonged to Isabella in London was not a problem however, Bella and Luce needed to discuss how he felt about the Paris apartment. It had belonged to Joe. Should it be sold? Luce asked if she was uncomfortable at his home? He had lived there with his wife. Many of the things there had been purchased by her. Bella laughed. They both had lived before. It would be foolish to worry over such mundane things.

Several days after the wedding, they left for England. There was a visit with Jim's brother and sister-in-law, Lord and Lady Moody before moving on to London. Isabella delighted in sharing with Luce all the places she had come to love. They toured the city and the countryside, bought gifts for the family, and discussed what would be needed to prepare the London residence for Yvette and Josephine if that became necessary. London had been damaged during the last war. If there were another war, the damage could be much more significant. The one thing Isabella had not been able to do while she was there, was to give Captain John Stewart an answer to his request.

Bella was still battling with this decision when they returned to France. Lucien had gone on to the vineyard, and she had things to catch up on. Her work had been put on hold because of the wedding. She found that Yvette had already taken care of the majority of things. Her daughter had become quite the entrepreneur.

Several days later, there was a panicked call from Jim. He and Andrew had been in Berlin on business. They were arrested for being in a nightclub that catered to people with alternative lifestyles. The police were threatening them with long jail sentences. Jim had bribed a guard to let him use the phone. The only thing that Bella could think of was to make a call to Captain Stewart. "Was there anything he could do to help?"

Jim and Andrew had arrived back in Paris, bruised and shaken. They told Isabella that a German councilman had turned up at the jail, spoken to the police captain, and money had changed hands. He had suggested that they leave Germany as soon as possible. Foreigners, especially their kind, were no longer welcome. Bella was relieved to have them back safe. Their jailers had treated them roughly. Jim had two broken ribs, and Andrew had a black eye. Had they remained there, the mistreatment would have continued. Andrew had not been allowed to call the American Embassy. That was against the law, but that had not seemed to matter. Germany had become a law unto itself.

Isabella carried a new shipment of merchandise to the boutique in London. She had made an appointment to meet with Captain Stewart to thank him for Jim and Andrew's safe return. John, as Isabella now called him, denied any knowledge of what had happened. Bella thanked him anyway. She had experienced firsthand just how dangerous the world they lived in had become. While she still hated the idea that she would be keeping secrets from Luce, she agreed to help MI6. Perhaps the work they did, could stop the war. That was her fervent hope.

Isabella returned to Chateau des Bois. It had been a bachelor's home for years. Some things needed to be updated or changed. Luce had suggested that they move slowly on the major renovations. Bella agreed. If there were another war, the home would once again be vulnerable. It had managed to survive the last one. Hopefully, it could survive the next.

Luce told her about his parents. His father, a twin to Lucien's grandfather, had been killed at the beginning of WW1. When his mother passed, his grandfather raised him. As a young boy, Lucien had helped his grandpa, Maurice, take care of the vineyard. For several years before the war, the grapes had been decimated by worms, damage from the war almost finished them off.

Luce's grandfather had placed many antiques from the chateau in the champaign caves for protection against the bombing during WW1. Hundreds of people also gathered there for safety. It became a virtual underground city, with schools, a gymnasium, and mess halls among other things. They remained there for the duration of the conflagration. At the cost of many lives, women and children, including Luce, would slip out between the bombings and pick what grapes remained. They were able to produce a limited supply of champagne even in those terrible years. If there were to be another invasion, he intended to share the caves with the citizenry again.

The return of the vineyards after the war took patience and hard work, but his grandfather had lived to see the cuttings sprout and become mature enough to produce excellent grapes. Once again Epernay had become the heart of the Champagne District. If there were to be another war, and the vineyards suffered, Luce, like his grandfather, would begin again.

Thirty-Four

Chapter 34. 1938 Comes to a Close.

Travel in Europe was becoming more difficult. Isabella had found the boutique suppliers were having a hard time keeping up with the demand, especially if the merchandise must cross borders. People were spending their money as if there was no tomorrow. The thinking was, "Enjoy today, you never know what the future will bring." There had been a conference of European leaders in Munich trying to appease the Germans. Perhaps this could put a stop to the threat of war.

Luce and Bella were both working hard. Lucien had a banner year when it came to his grapes. He had been busy night and day for more than three weeks. Now, the bottles of champagne filled the caves. Isabella had traveled back and forth between Paris, London, and Epernay with side trips to Luxemburg and Holland. She had spoken to her jeweler in Amsterdam and to the Yves. In casual conversations, she inquired about any plans they had, should the Germans invade. Everyone was extremely cautious with their replies, but Bella could tell that they were scared.

Isabella's work for MI6 had not caused any problems. If anything, it had been rather dull. She had been schooled on maps of the continent, knowledge of munitions, and her German had been brought up to date with the latest slang or anything else that was not part of the ordinary conversations. She had transported documents, delivered a wireless radio, but all in all, not much had changed.

The only significant remodeling Bella had been made to the chateau was a slight update to the bathroom and small kitchen. Luce had clothing and things in the Paris apartment and the London townhouse. Isabella laughed about the fact they were living like gypsies, traveling from place to place. It was a work in progress just to coordinate their schedule so they could spend time together. They both had businesses that needed their personal attention.

Josephine was babbling away in both French and English. Yvette was pregnant, and there would be another grandchild in the upcoming year. Andrew and Jim had sold their property in Paris and bought a small cottage outside of London. They no longer felt safe in Europe. The firm they ran together was losing clients. Most of the countries where their company had business, were now under German control. 1938 was drawing to a close. Europe was holding its breath.

Thirty-Five

Chapter 35. A Declaration of War.

Christmas had come and gone. Luce and Bella would celebrate their first anniversary in June, and in April, Yvette and Lucien were the proud parents of a baby boy. They named him Maurice, after his great grandfather, who was also Luce's grandfather. They laughed over the "grandfather connections." Luce had become the grandfather to Yevette's children when he married Bella. They said, "Try explaining that to people."

Jose was not too sure how she felt about being upstaged by a sibling. Sometimes she liked him, and sometimes she would prefer that he went back to wherever he had come from. Isabella and Luce loved being grandparents. Their delight was clouded only by the thought of the approaching storm. Czechoslovakia was now in the hands of the Third Reich.

A report had caused great consternation at MI6. It was

thought that German U-boats were in the English Channel and could easily reach London. While this turned out to be a false alarm, officials took this opportunity to begin testing the early warning systems. Air-raid sirens that were to be a defense against the Luftwaffe were heard. Isabella and Luce had been quietly moving personal papers, jewelry and other items to England. Yevette and Lucien had been doing the same. No one knew how safe these things would be in London, but they would be safer there than in France. The most important things were placed in the cellar at the Moody estate.

Isabella had traveled to Belgium and Luxembourg. On a streetcar in Brussels, someone had slipped her essential maps. Munitions were being manufactured in German factories that had graduated from tractors to armaments. Their location was vital information. Bella delivered them to the Home Office. She had also spoken with the Yves. "If the chance came for them to leave Luxembourg, would they go?" Their reply was to ask, "Where could they go?" Isabella had no answer.

The grape harvest reflected the mood of the world. It had been one of the worst in years. There had been mold, or worms, too much rain or not enough rain. Whatever the reason, it would be a poor harvest. August had come and gone. September 1st saw a sneak attack and the occupation of Poland by the Germans. Two days later, France and England responded with a declaration of war.

Members of the Bousquet family arrived at Chateau des Bois to help. Many things were moved to the caves. A false wall was built. The vats were then put back. Someone would need to look closely to realize there had been a new addition. There was nothing that could be done to protect the vineyards that had been almost destroyed by the trench warfare and bomb craters the last war had brought to Epernay.

The farmer bid them goodbye and promised to do his best to care for everything. They thanked him and begged him to stay safe. With heavy hearts, Luce and Bella locked the doors to the chateau. Would this be the last time they would see their home? Would it survive? With tears in their eyes, they turned away and drove back to Paris. Luce and Lucien went to enlist. Isabella went to hug her daughter and grandchildren. She would take them to England if it became necessary.

Thirty-Six

Chapter 36. Fraternizing With the Enemy.

France was slowly being swallowed up by the Germans. Letters for Bella or Yevette from their husbands were few and far between. At the beginning of the war, the men had been able to return for short visits. Lucien was in England training to be a pilot, and Luce was a Captain in the French army. Yvette had been convinced to remove the children from Paris as the German Army advanced. They had stayed at the London townhouse initially, but if the bombing began in earnest, they would move to the Moody estate. Yvette could not understand why her mother had chosen to remain in France. Paris was now in the hands of the enemy.

Some people on the streets were openly hostile. Any of Luce's family that were still in the city, had turned their backs on her. It seemed as if, Isabella was fraternizing with the enemy. Her

Parisian boutique was still open and doing business.

The clothing rationing did not apply to the German officers who purchased French perfume or other things for their wives or girlfriends. Officers sitting around drinking and watching beautiful women modeling lingerie gave little thought as to what their conversations revealed. Some had left briefcases containing secret documents lying about. No one considered the gorgeous redheaded proprietor a threat or imagined that copies of cryptic reports of troop movements or military orders from German High Command might be sent on to Allied Headquarters.

The beautiful auburn hair was rather obvious, so she had it cut and wore it in a stylishly short bob. It made her look younger, and it was easier to tuck up under a wig when she needed to be incognito. Padding and shabby clothing helped as well.

There was a short-wave radio hidden in the hollowed-out space under the back seat of her car. It could be powered by the car's battery. The enemy had become good at locating radio signals. It was much more of a challenge if the messages came from different locations. Gas was rationed, but she would find the tank's content mysteriously increased from time to time. She never knew how the Resistance was able to do that, but it made it easier for her to move the car from place to place. Her excuse if stopped, was that she needed to pick up merchandise that was being prepared by seamstresses on the Left Bank. Bella was aware if caught, she would be jailed or worse. Her husband and son-in-law were fighting for the freedom of France. She would do the same.

A group of drunken officers were joking about one of the older generals. It seemed that he fancied himself as a great lover.

The problem was that he drank too much. He would order young women brought to his room, but if he found himself unable to perform, he would blame the woman and beat her unmercifully. He killed one in a drunken rage. They laughed and said, "With all that exertion and his bad heart, one of these days, he will drop dead." They thought it was funny. Bella gritted her teeth, turned away, and began picking up their glasses. She was stopped in her tracks when a familiar name was mentioned.

"General Von Spaatz has his eye on a new conquest. She is a bartender at one of the places he frequents. Poor girl. She is pretty. When he gets finished with them, if they survive, they are scarred for life. She is safe for a week or so. He has gone to Nazi headquarters in Berlin to receive a commendation. When he comes back, he will be ready to celebrate."

Isabella found that she had been holding her breath. Peter was here, in Paris. Not only that, but he had become a monster. He was a cruel and dangerous threat. Peter had always used sex to control women, but now he blamed them for his own inabilities. The officers found the situation hilarious. It made her sick. She wanted to strangle them. Instead, she poured fresh drinks for the men. Casually she remarked, "You don't need to go anywhere else to drink. Does the cute bartender give you free drinks at the…. what was the name of the bar?"

Thirty-Seven

Chapter 37. The Warning.

A plump dark-haired woman with a limp had entered and now sat in the dimmest corner of the bar. She nursed a beer and watched the bartender. When the girl took a break and went out back to smoke, she followed.

"Mademoiselle, do not turn around. Just listen. General Von Spaatz has taken a liking to you. You are in grave danger. You should leave Paris at once."

The girl kept smoking. As if speaking to herself, she said, "I can't. My sister is an invalid in a wheelchair and has two children. They live with me. General Von Spaatz provides us with extra ration cards. That helps me to feed them. I have no choice, I must stay. A girl refused the General's attention, and her whole family was arrested. No one knows what happened to them."

Isabella could see there was no easy answer to the problem.

One person might have been smuggled out of Paris, but someone in a wheelchair, with two children, was next to impossible. Even if she were able to accomplish it, the terrible threat would remain. The General had a ready supply of vulnerable young women. If this girl were removed, he would select another. Peter was the problem. As long as he was alive and in command, women were in danger. What was the solution? Think Bella, think.

Thirty-Eight

Chapter 38. Drivers, Drunks and Pills.

The upper echelons had their own drivers. The younger officers needed to hire cars. A driver called "The Algerian" was among their favorites. His ability to supply liqueur or other things that were hard to find made him extremely popular. He would hang around, talking and joking with the other military and civilian chauffeurs, waiting until their passengers were ready to leave. There was a lot of information to be gathered between the drivers and the drunks. What he learned was passed on to Isabella then forwarded to MI6.

Bella realized she was running out of time. Peter was due back by the end of the week. Isabella had spent hours going over different scenarios. The question remained, how to stop General Von Spaatz without endangering herself or someone else? She had an idea, but it would need the Algerian's co-operation. It wasn't perfect and depended on a lot of variables. If it didn't work, she had no backup plan.

Bella collect certain herbs. She ground them down and, using other ingredients as a stabilizer, formed pills. Her contact, the Algerian, was given instructions as to their use and told to market them immediately. Customers would find that thirty minutes after taking one and only one, they would experience enhance sexual prowess. He was to make sure the news of their wonders spread. Time was of the essence. The plan was for the unsuspecting young officer who drove for Von Spaatz to become aware of the pills and mention them to his superior.

Men were delighted, even bragged about the increase in their sexual performance. The demand for that particular item grew by leaps and bounds. The Algerian was making money hand over fist. The weekend was fast approaching, but the most critical piece of the puzzle was lacking. Peter's driver was not one of the clients. To make matters worse, the General came back early.

Chapter 39. A Special Package, a Broken Heel, and a Medical Emergency.

Once again, the brunet entered the bar and chose a seat in the darkest corner. This time, instead of watching the bartender, her attention was on General Peter Von Spaatz. Bella watched as he consumed beer after beer, followed with whiskey chasers. She had no idea what she could do if he decided to leave and take the girl with him. She felt utterly helpless.

A group of officers at the next table were loudly celebrating a birthday. The conversation turned to the availability of local prostitutes. Money was collected to provide the celebrant with one for the evening. They also suggested that he could use something special to enhance the experience. One of the men boasted that thirty minutes after taking a "magic pill", he had been able to take care of three women in one night. They would go and get him a pill from the Algerian. It would be a birthday to remember.

Isabella noticed that Peter had been listening intently to the conversation. The mention of a substance that would perhaps help with his problem intrigued him. As the group rose to leave, Von Spaatz asked them to inform his driver that he needed to speak with him. When the young man appeared, the General whispered something to him. He saluted and left.

Bella finished her beer, rose, and walked into the hallway as if to use the bathroom. Opening the back door, she stepped out into the yard where the cars and drivers waited patiently for their passengers. Her contact had been watching and waiting. He walked over to the edge of the drive to put out his cigarette. Checking to see, no one looking, he gave her the high sign. The General's driver had received a very special package. It had been prepared for him and him alone. Its contents were twice the strength of the regular pills. Between the alcohol and his weak heart, Peter would be in trouble shortly after taking it. He would never beat a woman again. A heart attack if it didn't kill him, would render him helpless. If he died, no one would suspect foul play. General Von Spaatz would be buried with full military honors, and young women could breathe easier, silently give thanks, and rejoice at his passing. Bella crossed her fingers and walked back inside. All she could do now was wait.

Peter rose, paid his bill, and left. The bartender was told that the General's driver would be picking her up in an hour and driving her to the hotel. It was vital for the safety of the girl and others that Isabella's plan worked. She must see the results for herself.

The driver had delivered the young woman to the lobby by the time Bella reached the hotel. She sat there, waiting for him to return from parking the limousine. Isabella walked past her and dropped her gloves. As she bent down to retrieve them, she whispered, "Meet me in the bathroom."

After checking to be sure they were alone, Bella took one of the younger woman's shoes. She beat it against the sink until the heel broke. "Show the driver this. Tell him you need to go home for another pair of shoes. Hopefully, this should give you a small window of time. Lord willing, it will be enough."

The young officer returned to find the bartender in tears. She explained that she had broken the heel of her shoe. It would be best if she went home to fetch another pair. He became agitated. He explained that there was not enough time. She must go upstairs immediately. General Von Spaatz had prepared for her visit. He was waiting for her. She limped as slowly as she could towards the elevator. Bella watched as the doors slid shut. The lights, indicating the different floors moved up and up until they stopped at the top. She had failed. She sat there, numb.

Suddenly the lobby became electrified. People sprang into action. Ordered were barked into phones. Senior officers crowded into the elevator and sent it racing to the top floor. When it returned, a terrified young woman, the driver, and the hotel manager spilled out. The girl searched frantically for the woman who had deliberately broken her shoe. She was nowhere to be seen.

The screaming of an ambulance grew louder the closer it came to the hotel. Before it had come to a complete halt, medical personnel were on their way to the top floor, followed by corpsmen with a stretcher.

An elderly woman with gray hair, stood watching from across the street as the stretcher was carried out and placed in the ambulance, followed by several officers, including General Von Spaatz's driver. Someone said that there was no need to hurry as the patient was beyond medical attention. The driver should meet them at the hospital to answer questions, but it seemed cut and dried. The General had a massive coronary, and nothing could have been done. Everyone knew that he had a bad heart.

The old lady limped away and was swallowed up by the dark. A young woman with a broken heel hobbled off in the other direction. The ambulance, siren wailing, dashed off into the night.

Chapter 40. Compromised.

The next day, all the talk at the boutique was of the heart attack that General Von Spaatz had suffered. His military driver and a woman had entered the room the night before and found him unconscious. An ambulance had been called, but it was too late. He had died on the way to the hospital. No one seemed surprised, and no one suspected foul play.

A week or two had passed. Isabella had been waiting to see if there would be an inquiry. The war had heated up. America had joined the fight. No one seemed too worried about the death of one drunken General. There was so much more to concern the Nazi hierarchy.

Bella had been sending information nightly to London. Things were changing rapidly. Troops were being sent to hold positions that seemed in danger of being overrun. Fronts were so fluid, that soldiers sometimes found themselves behind enemy lines. Plans were written, cancelled, then rewritten only to be changed hours later. Her job became more precarious. Her sources were drying up.

The boutique had been virtually empty for days. There was nothing to report. Most of the officers had been sent to the front. Those that were still in Paris were at headquarters working on battle plans. Bella was considering her options. Perhaps it was time for her to leave.

The Algerian was becoming agitated and even threatening. Her contact had enjoyed the extra income created by the sale of the pills. He saw no reason for her to stop making them unless, as he insinuated, her goal had been to kill Von Spaatz. Isabella warned him of his complicity. No one must suspect that Peter's death was anything but natural. If the plot were revealed, she would not be the only one found guilty. The Algerian muttered something under his breath and sulked off.

She was using the backroom at the boutique as a bedroom ever since the Germans had taken over her apartment. The only thing she had been allowed to remove had been her personal belongings, and some clothes. Her jewelry and valuables were safe in England.

Bella had only been asleep for an hour or two. Something or someone woke her. She reached under her pillow for the pistol hidden there. A man's voice whispered, "Listen. You have been compromised. There was an anonymous tip. The Gestapo know about you. You will be tortured for information, tried as a spy and shot. Hurry, there is a truck waiting outside."

Isabella threw on a dress and her shoes, grabbed a coat, her purse, and the gun, and followed him out through the window. As they raced down the alley, the sound of police sirens, could be heard. There was an old bread truck parked around the corner, with the motor idling. They climbed in, and the truck, It's headlights off, drove away slowly.

Forty-One

Chapter 41. England at Last.

Since leaving the city, Isabella had been passed from one group to another. Sometimes it was a single man or woman. Sometimes there were four or five people involved. She had traveled in the bread truck, an old car, on a motorcycle, and walked. The shoes she had worn when she escaped were long gone. A pair of old army boots were rubbing blisters on her heels. If she managed to sleep, her dreams were of food and a long hot bath.

Once they had left Paris, the war had become all too real. Life in the city had been precarious and uncomfortable, but nothing like the terrible, dangerous, and cruel world that awaited her. People were starving. Little children wandered around aimlessly or sat staring into space. Whole towns were nothing but burning broken rubble. Bloated animal carcasses lay in the fields where they had been killed. People, that had been lined up against a wall and shot, lay where they had fallen. There was no one left alive in the village to bury them.

There had been several close calls, but at last she arrived back in England. She reported to MI6. They had been informed of her betrayal. A caller had exposed her to the Gestapo as a spy. The Algerian was the prime suspect. She had been the only one he dealt with so, none of her companions were in danger of being caught. Isabella's concern was that there would be repercussions for the Bousquet family.

Isabella and Yvette had never changed their last names on the lease for the business. It still read Madam and Mademoiselle Dean. Hopefully, because they did not have her married name, Luce's family would be safe from persecution for her actions. Most of them were no longer in Paris. The Germans were being pressed hard from all sides by the Allies. That might keep them from spending too much time combing through the records looking for connections to her.

Her usefulness to MI6 was over. She would receive a medal for her service to the country at some point, but for now she was once again just a citizen. Yvette thought her mother was both brave and insane for what she had done. Bella had given her a carefully censored version of her work in France. Yvette was upset to see how thin her mother had become during the escape, and there was a white streak in the front of her hair. Bella didn't tell her about the scar that ran across her back from a bullet that had grazed her while she was fleeing from the enemy.

Isabella could not believe how much her grandchildren had grown since she had seen them last. Her granddaughter was delighted to have her "Nanna" back. Maurice had been so young when he left for England, that he didn't remember Bella.

It had taken a day or two before he decided that this person was someone he liked. Soon he had claimed her for his own, much to the chagrin of his sister.

Forty-Two

Chapter 42. A Miracle Revealed.

There were two letters waiting for her in England from Luce. It had been months since they had been written. Much of it had been blacked out by the sensors. There was no way of knowing where in Europe, he was and if he was still all right. Yvette's husband was in the Forces Aeriennes Francaises Libres. The Free French Air Corps flew out of the R.A.F. Base in Elvington, England, so he was able to call her from time to time. Baby Maurice would soon have his first birthday and her son-in-law was hoping to be there to celebrate. How wonderful it would be if she could see Luce and to be sure he was safe. The blessing was, that she had not received the dreaded letter saying he had been killed.

Isabella had settled into her townhouse in London. Blocks of flats had been damaged all around, but so far Bella's had escaped the bombing. People were adjusting to leaving their homes and spending the night in the shelters. The Londoners opened their hearts to the military. If you had a spare room, you welcomed these brave youngsters when they needed a place to stay for a night or two. Bella was no exception to this unwritten rule. Maude's grandson George was a frequent visitor any time he had a weekend pass, and often brought a friend with him. Lady Moody had always welcomed Isabella and her daughter into her home. She delighted to return the favor.

Bella was expecting George Moody and one of his buddies. The fireplace was in full blaze and the tea and a few cakes were ready for their arrival. She had gone to change her shoes when she heard the front door open. George called out to let her know that they were there. Isabella started down the stairs. "Aunty, we're here. This is my pal. He is from America. His name is…" There was no need to finish the sentence. Bella had taken one look, and she knew his name, Joseph Dean. She missed the last two steps when she fainted.

Isabella returned to consciousness, to find two anxious young men staring down at her. They had carried her to the couch and now hovered over her wondering what to do. When she began to cry, they were even more upset.

Bella had dried her eyes and was sipping a cup of tea. She was still in shock. All the years since Joe's death, she had grieved the loss of her baby, yet here he was. She had taken one look at him and knew. He was the spitting image of his father. What she did not understand, was how this was possible. Isabella assured the two young men that she was fine. She would give them an explanation for why she had fainted, but first, would Joseph answer a few questions about his family in America?

He told her that he had been raised by his grandfather after his mother and father were killed in an automobile accident.

When America had entered the war, and after the attack on Pearl Harbor, he had enlisted despite his grandfather's objections. His father had been a pilot during the last war and had been wounded. He had even lost an eye. Joseph had wanted to follow in his footsteps and be a pilot. When the army discovered that he was color blind, the wish to fly was denied. Instead, his job was to make sure that the planes were fit to fly. "Why is this important?" he asked.

Bella rose and took a photo album from the drawer. Opening it, she pointed to a photo, that showed Joe in his uniform. Joseph couldn't understand why this woman had his father's picture. That same photo sat on his grandfather's desk. Isabella turned the page to reveal wedding photos. There were more pages, showing Joe with Bella and some with Yvette. After the one showing a pregnant Isabella with Joe in Brighton, the photos stopped. The young man sat there staring at the album, and then at Bella. This woman was saying that his mother was not dead. How could that be?

Bella fought back the tears as she told her son the story that led up to his being taken to America. They had told her that her baby and his father were dead, and the bodies were shipped to the States for burial. Exactly how his grandfather and the lawyers had been able to accomplish such a horrendous trick was a mystery. His grandfather had had a heart attack and died while Joseph was in basic training, and the lawyers had passed away years before. There was no one left to answer the questions.

George confirmed that he had heard his dad and uncles talk about Joe, but it never occurred to him that his buddy's father and the Joe they spoke of, was the same person. There were group photos of the Moody family with Joe in attendance. He had never asked how Joseph's father had died. What were the odds of them ever meeting? If he hadn't brought his friend to stay at Bella's, they both would have gone to their graves without knowing the other existed.

Forty-Three

Chapter 43. Happiness, and Hospitals.

Joseph was coming to grips with the fact that his grandfather had lied to him all those years and kept him from his mother. His mother was furious remembering how she had suffered thinking her son was dead. There was no way to make up for all the time she had missed. Bella had been taught to forgive those who trespass against you, but to steal someone's baby and tell them it had died… that was unforgivable.

Yvette was ecstatic to find out that her brother was not only alive, but here in England. Joe was amazed to find out he had a sister, a niece and a nephew. When he managed to get a pass, he spent it with his newly discovered family. His mother, Isabella, found herself experiencing a roller coaster of emotions. She was on top of the world one moment, rejoicing in the presence of her son, and in anger and despair the next, remembering how he had been taken from her.

Her pleasure in finding young Joe, was cut short when, she received the notification that Luce had been wounded. He had been shipped back and was in an Army hospital in the north of England. She arrived, to find him lying in bed, his leg in traction, his head shaved completely. and the left side of it bandaged. The jeep that Luce had been riding in, had been hit. It rolled over and caught fire. He had managed to crawl out from under it but had suffered a badly broken leg and his ear had been damaged by the explosion that followed. They had stitched up his head and the ear at a field hospital. The damage meant that he would be deaf in the left ear for the rest of his life. He had a few burns, but they were superfluous. Isabella didn't know whether to laugh or cry. Her husband looked so sad, with a shaved head and a singed eyebrow, but for her, Luce had never looked more handsome. He was alive. That was all that mattered. Bella could not wait to tell him about Joseph.

Lucien stared at her in disbelief. Bella's son was alive and here in England? What kind of miracle was that? He knew that Isabella had lost not only her husband, but her baby in a terrible accident. The bodies had been sent back to America. While she had never said so, Luce knew how much she had suffered, and grieved over the loss of her child. Now the impossible had happened, Bella had her son back. There was an other surprise for everyone, Yvette was pregnant with twins.

Until Lucien could be released, Isabella would spend most of her time at the hospital. They were shorthanded and appreciated the extra help. She had rented a ground floor flat, close by. It would make it easier for him, while he needed to maneuver on crutches and with his leg in a cast. It was going to be a while before he would be free to leave. Once he was given a clean bill of health, she would take him home, but for now, knowing he was safe was enough. Luce was having terrible nightmares and suffered from what the doctors called shell shock. He was jumpy, would have outbursts of anger or fall into a deep depression. Yvette and the children had also moved north to escape the intense bombing and were living close by and could visit. At first, the children's loud noises were a problem, but now, most of the time, he was able to laugh at their antics. Gradually, he adjusted to the fact that for him the fighting was probably over. He prayed that soon, it would be over for everyone. Isabella's prayer was that the twins be born into a peaceful world.

Forty-Four

Chapter 44. A Reluctant Hero.

The children, and Yvette had remained up north where the bombers could not reach them. Bella had taken Luce back to London. He would be checking in with the hospital from time to time to be sure he was continuing to heal. Bella had told him of her involvement with MI6 in Paris. Luce was upset and angry with her for putting herself in danger. Isabella's explanation that she had been contributing to the war effort just as he and his nephew had, fell on deaf ears. He had thought her safe in Britain, but instead she had been risking her life in France. It would take him a long time to forgive her for what he considered a terrible deception. She didn't tell him of her involvement in General Von Spaatz death. There are somethings that cannot be shared, not even with those you love.

Maurice had celebrated his first birthday in style. Not only was his father able to be there, but his grandpa Luce, his Nanna, and his new uncle. Everyone had come up from London, and Joseph had been able to liberate some oranges from the mess hall. The children had never seen oranges and were fascinated by them. Josie had eaten two, despite Yvette's warnings. The little girl spent the rest of the evening throwing up. That was a small distraction to a wonderful day. All too soon Joseph and Lucien were on their way back to the base. Yvette, Bella and Luce, were trying to stay upbeat, but the fact that the two men were going back to the war had reminded them of the ever-present dangers.

Lucien and his squadron had gone out on a bombing run. Bella was very thankful that Joe was at the base, rather than in the air being shot at, then the news came over the radio. There had been a raid on the airstrip. Many of the planes were damaged and there were huge casualties among the ground crews. It was too soon to tell how many were dead or wounded. Bella's only thought was, "Would God have sent her son back to her, only to snatch him away? Could God be that cruel?"

The military were asking everyone to stay away while they assessed the damage and gathered information. They would be publishing lists of the living and the dead as soon as it was available. It took three long agonizing days before Isabella knew that her son was among the living. There had been so many casualties, they had been dispersed to different hospitals. That made it harder to verify who had survived the attack. Her son-in-law, Lucien Bousquet had called as soon as he knew where Joseph was, and that he was alive. Bella needed to see for herself that her son was all in one piece. She and Luce arrived at the hospital, to find Joe sitting up in bed, flirting with the pretty young nurse that was feeding him. His hands and arms were bandaged, and there was a rakish slash on one cheek. It had made him look even more like his father.

George Moody had gone to visit his parents on a weekend pass so he had not been on the base when the raid began. Joseph had been taking a cigarette break when the planes arrived. At first, he thought it was the squadron returning, but then the bombs began raining down. Planes on the runways, some full of fuel, burst into flame. Sheets of molten metal flew in all directions. Huge holes appeared on the tarmac. Men, their clothing on fire, ran screaming. The noise and the smell was incredible. Smoke, fuel, tar, burning flesh, and other unknowns mixed, making him nauseous. The night was an eerie shade of red with flashes of blinding light whenever a plane exploded. The enemy delivered their payload and disappeared into the night.

A soldier ran towards him, burning clothes lit up his face. Joe grabbed a tarp, threw it over him, and wrestled him to the ground, beating out the flames. Someone was caught beneath what appeared to be a large piece of wing. Joseph lifted it long enough for the man to struggle out, never realizing that the hot metal was burning his hands. Once the soldier was clear, Joe half dragged, half carried him to an area behind the sandbags where he had deposited the first burn victim. Joseph rescued three more, before it occurred to him, that the Allied planes coming back from their raid would have no clear place to land. Not all the landing strips were damaged by the bombing, but all were covered with debris. Large slabs of what had once been planes, lay everywhere. Anyone attempting to put their aircraft down on that would encounter certain death.

Joe found a bulldozer and climbed aboard. He dropped the blade, headed for the first runway, and began pushing the wreckage off to the sides. Others saw what he was attempting to do and followed suit. Where they lacked bulldozers, men were beginning to clear the debris by any means possible. Soon the smoke-covered field was filled with a swarm of people. The field must be cleared, so they would clear it. The incoming planes had a rough landing, but not one pilot was lost, including Lucien Bousquet.

Joseph never knew how long he drove the bulldozer. Someone had taken his place when he collapsed from smoke inhalation. He came to in the hospital, with a terrible headache, his hands swaddled in bandages. People were saying he was a hero. Joe had rescued men and orchestrated the clearing of the airstrip, saving people, pilots, and planes. Like his father before him, he felt that he didn't deserve to be called a hero. Others thought differently.

Forty-Five

Chapter 45. England Will Not Go Down Without a Fight.

Isabella had invited Captain John Stewart to supper and to meet Luce. She no longer worked for MI6, but she and John had become friends. Bell had discreetly left the two of them alone with their drinks after they finished eating. The men talked about the war, and how terrible the bombing had become. Luce felt guilty not to be still fighting, even though his shattered leg was slow to heal. John remarked on the possibility of there being something Luce might do at the home office. Talk then turned to Isabella's intelligence work in Paris. Captain Stewart praised her contributions. He explained that the work she had done was indefinable. Her access to enemy secrets and documents had given them information they were unable to collect anywhere else. Without her help, more battles and men would have been lost. The country owed her a great debt. Luce should be proud of his wife.

John was preparing to leave when Joseph came in. He was unable to work on the planes, with his hands still bandaged, so he had been given a desk job in the quartermaster's office. Luce told John of the raid on the airstrip and Joseph's heroic actions, much to Joe's embarrassment. Captain Stewart laughed and made the comment that heroism ran in the family.

While they stood talking, the sirens began their wail, the barrage balloons went up and the searchlights lit up the night sky. Taking their gas masks, they made the trip to the shelter. Just before they reached the steps to the underground, the first bombs began to fall. When finally, the "all clear siren" sounded, they emerged from the shelter to find London in ruins. The firetrucks and the ambulances were finding it impossible to traverse the streets. Even if they could have picked up patients, hospitals were in shambles. London lay groaning like a wounded beast. Flames, smoke, and the wailing of sirens were in stark contrast to the people standing around in dazed silence. Buildings lay on top of buildings, it was impossible to tell where one street ended, and another began. There had been bombings before, but this had been a living hell.

John had gone to check on his office and his men. Bella and Luce found a place to rest, while Joseph went off to see how the flat had fared, or even if there was a flat. Medics were performing triage anywhere they could, and people carried the wounded through the debris to a hastily erected first aid station. Isabella went to help. Soon, those who could, were searching through the rubble for anyone trapped underneath. Luce borrowed a notebook from a policeman and began collecting the names of the wounded, the dead, and the dying. His war experience had given him insight into the importance of being able to identify bodies. Someone would be looking for them. Families would need this information.

It had taken hours, but Joseph had found his way back. There were whole areas of London that were still burning, with huge mounds of rubble, buildings in different stages of collapse, and furniture hanging precariously in space awaiting their trip to oblivion. There would be areas that seemed untouched until you realized that some of the windows had been blown out by the compression from the explosions. Bella's flat was still standing. He had stopped long enough to be sure it was secured, then returned to Isabella and Luce.

The police and medics had joined Luce in collecting names. Bulletin boards were put up where names could be checked, or families could ask for help in locating a loved one. Captain Stewart had set Luce up with a basement office where he compiled the names. He would work until he was exhausted, sleep for an hour or two, then take up the impossible task again. Isabella helped the medics or worked in the soup kitchens, and Joseph returned to the base.

Night after night, wave after wave of planes blanketed the sky, dropping their deadly cargo on England. The subway stations had become home to hundreds of exhausted, hungry, unwashed bodies. People had brought in wireless radios, so they could hear messages from King George, Winston Churchill, and others. Little children wore their Micky Mouse gas masks. There were singalongs and storytelling, musicians brought their instruments and played, couples married, strangers became friends for life, babies were born, and deaths occurred. The circle of life went on, even there in the crowded bowels of the earth.

When the bombing ceased for a few hours, wheelbarrows

would appear from nowhere and people began removing bricks and rubble from the streets. Teams hunted for the living or the dead trapped beneath collapsed buildings. Vegetables were liberated from victory gardens to feed the masses. Using small carts, bicycles, or on foot, farmers delivered chickens, eggs, and milk for the children. The whole country was being beaten to its knees, but the British, like their Bulldogs, were too stubborn to admit defeat. After weeks and weeks of this Blitzkrieg, with city after city almost destroyed, it suddenly stopped. England held its breath. Some worried that the invasion was imminent. Coastal inhabitants loaded their shotguns and barred their doors. Any stranger was looked on with suspicion. If the Germans came, they were ready. England would not go down without a fight.

Forty-Six

Chapter 46. Peace at Last.

Joseph's hands had healed long ago but would never have the dexterity they once had. He received a promotion and was assigned to work with the military reconnaissance checking out the maps. It was the fact that he was color blind that allowed him to see beyond the camouflage that fooled others. Shapes of buildings or anything else, in the photos, would be clear to him. That gave the bombers the information they needed to destroy munition factories, military headquarters, and air bases. Joseph, in his spare time, had taken up black and white photography and was becoming well known. His photos of war-torn England and its people had been featured in newspapers and magazines. When there was no longer any need for his services, he would be mustered out either in Britain or America. The choice would be his. While he could go back to America and join his uncle and cousins in his grandfather's firm, that didn't appeal to him. He didn't think it would appeal to them either.

The twins had been born just as the war appeared to be drawing to an end. In Europe, city after city had been liberated. The Free French had entered Paris once more, to cheering crowds. German military were retreating or surrendering. The war in Europe was over. The Japanese were still holding fast to all they had captured, and the fighting was fierce. Men were dying from the heat and diseases as well as the war. Much to his mother's dismay, orders had come through for Joseph to be deployed to the Philippines.

The day Joseph had come to tell them goodbye, he found his orders had been canceled. A terrible thing called an atomic bomb had fallen on a place called Hiroshima, and another on Nagasaki. No one understood how destructive these bombs were, or how many people had died, but the war with Japan had come to an abrupt end.

Andrew and Jim's little cottage in the English countryside had been spared, as had the little tea shop they ran. Isabella's London flat had not been as fortunate. The most important things had been removed to the basement at the Moody estate, but the townhouse and all the beautiful furnishings were gone. "Things can be replaced, people can't." was Bella's answer when informed of the loss. She and Luce had no idea how their home and vineyard near Epernay had fared. The war was over, but it would be a while before they could travel to France. The apartment in Paris was probably not damaged but what shape would it be in? What about Yvette and Lucien's home on the outskirts of the city? So many questions without answers, but they were all safe. That was the only thing that mattered. The family didn't know what the future held, but they counted their blessings and would deal with it together.

Chapter 47. A Long Held Grudge.

Yvette and Lucien arrived in France and found that their home had been used as a hospital for German soldiers. The house was overrun with fleas, and rats were everywhere. Most of the furnishings were ruined, but the building stood firm. After removing the bedding, exterminating the vermin, and airing out the house, they set about cleaning and painting. It would take a while, but the property would be made livable once more.

Lucien wasn't sure if or when there would be a need for a new automobile dealership, besides, he had loved flying. There were rumors of startup airlines, and they would want pilots. He intended to be first in line for the job. Yvette had her hands full with the four children, and the house renovations. She would wait to see how things went before thinking of starting another business.

Isabella's apartment in Paris was a mess. Graffiti marked up the walls. Most of the beautiful furnishings were gone. Apparently, the piano had been too big to steal, but anything of value that could be carried off, was no longer there. The bedroom had been stripped except for the largest chest-of-drawers. It looked as if Joe's antique bed had been disassembled and hauled away. The bedclothes lay in sad heaps on the floor where they had been dropped. Perhaps the Germans had taken everything on their way out of town, or perhaps thieves, knowing the apartment was now unoccupied had helped themselves. Curtains for the most part, seemed to be intact. Some paint and new furniture would make it livable again. Did they want to remain in Paris? That was the question.

Isabella went to check on the boutique. The windows had been broken, and everything inside had been smashed or stolen. There was nothing worth keeping left. Dreadful things had been written on the walls. The French people never realized that she was working for the Allies. If she cared to rebuild her business, the first thing she must do is to prove her innocence. People must be convinced that she had not collaborate with the Nazis. Bella needed to find a way to do that, or she wouldn't be able to live in Paris, let alone have a business there.

As she turned to leave, a shadow fell across the doorway. The Algerian stood there staring at her, a look of triumph on his face. "I knew if I waited, you would come back." His face was full of hate, his grin was more like a grimace. "You left me to the Germans. They tortured me for information. I was blamed for everything you did. They beat me, pulled out my teeth, broke my fingers and applied electric wires to my genitals. They wanted information that I didn't have. They didn't believe me. When they were done with me, they threw me in an open grave with other prisoners and left me to die. I couldn't die until I had punished you for what you did. You left me to suffer."

He stood, blocking the doorway. Isabella was trapped. She realized if she retreated back into the building, she would be in more danger. If she screamed for help, would anyone hear her? Was there anything that she could use for a weapon? If he came towards her, could she get passed him and to the door? Bella tried to reason with him. "I am sorry for what happened to you, but you are the one who turned me in to the Gestapo. If you hadn't done that, they would never have known about you." That was the wrong thing to say.

His scream of anger chilled her to the bone. "I will kill you, you bitch. I will slice you up one piece at a time until you beg for mercy, the same way I did." Suddenly there was a knife in his hand, and he lunged at her. Bella dodged as the blade came down. She thrust out her purse to protect herself. The knife grazed her arm, pierced the leather bag and came out the other side. He wrestled with removing the blade from the purse. It slowed him down for a moment. That was all Bella needed. She raced for the open door. The Algerian shook the knife loose, grab her, and raising the blade, "I'll kill you!" he roared. A shot rang out, the man hung suspended for a moment, then crumpled to the floor. Luce stood there, a gun in his hand.

Everything had happened so fast. It seemed unreal. Isabella collapsed into Luce's arms. The shot had caused people on the street to stop in their tracks. A gendarme was summoned. He took one look at the body on the floor and demanded to know what had happened. Luce admitted to having shot the attacker to protect his wife. The officer then turned to question Bella. "Had she known the man, and did she know why he had attacked her." Isabella was beginning to shake as the shock of what had happened, set in. Luce pointed to the knife on the floor, and the cut on Bella's arm, as well as the hole in the purse. Her dress was badly torn where the Algerian had tried to stop her. It seemed obvious that she had been the victim and was in no shape to answer questions. With the policeman's permission, he would take his wife to have her wound dressed. Bella was beginning to feel faint from lose of blood. She needed a doctor. They would both appear at the police station later to give their statement. After taking their personal identification, he gave them an appointment and emphasized the necessity of their punctual appearance. There would be grave consequences if his orders were ignored. Luce had taken a taxi to the shop. The driver had waited, and now drove them both to the hospital.

Isabella had finally stopped shaking. Back at the hotel where they had been staying, she had changed her clothes, and after a small brandy, the two of them left for the police station. Upon arrival, they were amazed to find newspaper reporters everywhere. After Isabella had given her statement to the police captain, along with her involvement during the war with MI6 as the reason the Algerian had attacked her, an inquiry was wired to England. Once her statement was corroborated by London, she and Luce were cleared of all charges. Her story became the headline in every paper, in both countries. Luce was hailed as her savior. She too, was hailed as a heroine, someone who had helped with the war effort. Parisians no longer believed she had worked for the Nazis. Isabella had found a most unexpected way to clear her name. If she decided to rebuild her business in Paris, she could. Now it was time for them both to go home.

Forty-Eight

Chapter 48. Chateau des Bois.

The driveway to their home was almost unrecognizable. A guardhouse stood by the gatepost. The gate, hanging by one hinge, stood open. Barbed wire in twists deformed the top of the stone fence. The parkland was sadly overgrown. No chickens or cows decorated the landscape. Chateau de Bois seemed deserted. As they grew nearer, they could see that the building was still intact. They gave a sigh of relief. When the car drew up to the entrance, an old man with a crutch, emerged. It wasn't until he spoke that they recognized the farmer. The last time they had seen Louis, he was a plump happy man with a full head of hair and a big grin. This thin, balding, sad man bore no resemblance to the person they had said goodbye to so long ago.

They had brought a picnic basket full of food with them. It was to hold them over until they knew if the house was livable. They immediately began to share the contents with Louis. Between bites, he told them what had expired since their last meeting.

The German Army had used the chateau as headquarters for the wine-growing region. Unlike the previous war, when the vineyards had been completely destroyed, they had been cared for and used to produce the champagne that the district was famous for. Prisoners of war, persons from the concentration camps, and other forced laborers were brought in to do the hard work of caring for the grapes. Done by hand, the labor was grueling, and the limited food rationing caused many to fall by the wayside. Even the horses were unable to keep up the pace. Oxen were conscripted from other villages to do the work.

Any person who had worked the vineyard and knew anything about the production of champagne, if found, was put to work. This included the farmer and his family. The war years saw the grapes flourish. At first the wine was bootlegged, reminding some of the Prohibition in America, but then distribution became more organized. Champagne was sent back to Germany to the higher-ranking members of the Third Reich, the rest was sold to the neutral countries that still did business with the Nazis. There was even champagne bearing the label, "Reserve a la Wehrmacht". It was a great money maker for the conquerors.

Persons found to be sabotaging the work, or trying to stall the production, even if they owned the vineyards were shipped off to Auschwitz or Buchenwald. Heads of many of the grand champagne houses found themselves in concentration camps. Not all of them survived.

When the Germans realized that the Allies were just hours

away, they hastily loaded men, champagne, and the healthiest of the prisoners into the trucks. Fearing the worst, they left everything and everyone else behind and headed for the German frontier. Some of the remaining workers approached the chateau with the intention of burning it to the ground. Louis retrieved his shotgun from its hiding place and facing the group, explained that the persons who owned the house and the vineyard, were French, fighting for France. They deserved, to find their home intact when they returned. Lucien and Isabella could think of nothing they could say or do to repay him for his service.

Bella asked him how he and his family had managed during the war. He sat in silence, his head bowed, then slowly and painfully he began, "It wasn't too bad at first. My son had gone to join the army. My wife, my young daughter, and I were not harmed. They needed everyone to help with the vineyard. We were forced to give up our home and live in the caves with the prisoners. Food was a problem. We worked long days, with short rations."

He paused for a moment, then continued, "Love knows no difference between enemies and allies. A young German soldier fell in love. He would sneak food to my daughter. When his commanding officer was notified of his collaboration, as an example to the troops, he was shot in front of my pregnant child. She went into labor hours later and bled to death giving birth to a stillborn baby. My wife never spoke again. Two weeks later, she took her own life. We buried the three of them in the graveyard we had made in the garden. Others are buried there." Bella's tears ran freely as she listened to his story, but the farmer had no more tears to shed. "I am not sure if my son is still alive. All I can do is hope and pray. Perhaps he will come back. Perhaps not."

Forty-Nine

Chapter 49. The Brotherhood of Survival.

⚜

The Germans had electrified the chateau. There was a large generator for emergency outages. Telephone lines had been installed, and plumbing had been updated as well. Cosmetically the finished installation was laughable. Plywood panels were tacked up over the holes in the walls where the wires had been run. In many rooms, bare bulbs were the only lighting. Things were practicable, not decorative. Bella lost count of all the desks, typewriters, and phones. Everything needed to run the operation was left where it had been used. Papers had been burned in large barrels and fireplaces. Smoke had marked up the walls, and a large area of the parquet floor in the ballroom had been burned. The roof had been repaired after it had begun to leak, but the wall and ceiling still bore the stains. The farmer's rooms were filled with army cots for use by the soldiers, and Joe's bedroom and office had housed the officers.

The prisoners that remained, were in poor shape. Most were in such terrible condition, that there was no hope of their surviving. Luce and Isabella did their best to make their last days as comfortable as possible. The little graveyard grew daily, but with better food and care, some recovered. Several left to find their homes and their families. Five stayed, to help with the care and restoration of Chateau de Boise and the vineyard. They lived with the farmer, who welcomed the company. Men who had shared forced labor and starvation now shared the brotherhood of survival.

As the men began returning from the war, Luce gathered a group together to help with the harvest when the grapes ripened. The Germans lacked knowledge or didn't care when it came to keeping the machinery in good shape. Much of the equipment needed repair. One of the prisoners of war had been an engineer. His help was invaluable. Parts were hard to find. He managed to repair or manufacture something that worked, and soon, he had things running. With care, they would be able to harvest the grapes, and make champagne. The biggest drawback was the lack of bottles. That problem was solved by having the distributors bring their own bottles to be exchanged. While it wasn't their best year, champagne flowed once again in Epernay manufactured by the French. Luce felt that his grandfather would have been proud.

Fifty

Chapter 50. Time Flies.

How quickly the years had passed. The children were growing so fast, it was almost impossible to keep up with them. The twins, Dean and Davidia loved visiting with their Papa and Nanna at the vineyard. Josephine had become an accomplished ballerina and was eager to join a ballet company upon graduation. Maurice was fascinated with anything mechanical and was always taking things apart to see what made them tick. Sometimes he even put them back together.

Isabella and Luce were happily ensconced at Chateau des Boise. Bella worked for years restoring the chateau. The fact that the Germans had installed electricity and updated the plumbing had been an unexpected bonus. The chandeliers in the dining room and the ballroom reflected beautifully in the mirrors. The parquet floors had been refinished, and portraits, recovered from the hidden compartment in the caves, hung on the walls. Bella purchased rugs, added to the furniture, and made curtains for each room. The huge new kitchen was more than capable of preparing enough food for the Bousquet family gatherings, or for all the extra hands brought in for the grape harvest.

Their small vineyard made a name for itself in the world of wines. The label "Chateau de Boise" was sought after by champagne connoisseurs. Both General de Gaulle and General Eisenhower had enjoyed a bottle or two. It had taken several years to bring the vineyard back to its peak production. The problem was the lack of decent equipment rather than the abundance of grapes. All but one of the men, who had remained at the chateau, had passed, and they were buried in the little graveyard. The farmer had lived long enough to see his son return from the prisoner-of-war camp. The son was now raising his family in the carriage house. He and his boys were welcome hands during the harvesting and champagne production.

Bella's son, Joseph Dean had become a renowned photographer and traveled the world taking photos of people and places. He owned a wonderful gallery in London and one in New York. His family in America had managed to run his grandfather's business into the ground. The young cousins were big on spending but not on working. They had quickly run through their inheritance, unlike Joe, who had made good use of his.

He had met a beautiful young actress while working in Spain. They were married at the chateau, much to the delight of his mother and Luce. They had two children, a boy and a girl. Bella wished they lived closer and not in New York but travel between countries was becoming easier. She and Luce had been to America, and Joseph's family had spent summers at the chateau. Isabella was never happier than when her grandchildren were there and playing hide and seek in the secret passageways. She would join in, much to their delight. You are never too old to play hide and seek.

Fifty-One

Chapter 51.. Becoming a Vintner.

Josephine had become a premier ballerina, and Maurice had graduated with an engineering degree. Dean and Davidia were entering college and Joe's children, Maria and Marcus were both at Julliard. They had all helped in the vineyard from time to time, but Davidia was the child most interested in the care of the grapes. She would watch and listen as Luce and the vintners would debate the best way to make champagne, the temperature needed, the fermentation solution, the need for bacteria, and the best way to clean the vats. Before she was twelve, Davidia knew the names and the look of the different grapes that went into the finished product. The sciences she would study in college were to help advance the quality of the wine. She and Luce would spend hours discussing how to produce the most champagne from their grapes. At first, her being young and a female was a problem, but soon Davidia had earned the grudging respect of the older male vintners.

Time was slowing Luce down. The hearing problem in his left ear had been joined by his right ear. Years of the insistent thwack of the grape pressing machines had stolen what hearing he had left. His leg troubled him when the weather was damp. By the end of the harvesting and the bottling of the finished champagne, he was exhausted. He hated to admit it, but he was looking forward to the time when he could step back and turn the vineyard over to Davidia. While women vintners were rare, there were a few. She was the obvious choice to continue the family business. She would have graduated by the next year's harvest and would take up residence at Chateau des Bois. Isabella was happily remodeling a wing of the house for her private use.

Fifty-Two

Chapter 52. As Time Goes By.

Davidia had been running the vineyard for several years. At first, Luce had been there to talk everything over with, but as time went by, she needed his help less and less. He had suffered a slight stroke which had made it hard for him to walk. He spent a great deal of time sitting in the garden and admiring the flowers that Isabella had planted. The parkland had been landscaped and trees now lined the drive. Beautiful flowerbeds and shrubbery made the approach to the chateau even more welcoming and picturesque.

The other grandchildren spent less and less time at the chateau. They were all leading such busy lives. Josephine was usually on tour or preparing for a new ballet. Maurice owned his own successful business and was engaged to be married. Dean was preparing to take the bar. They would have a lawyer in the family. Joseph's son was touring Europe. There were several large orchestras to which he had sent his resume. He had wanted to work in France or Italy for several years before returning to the States. His sister was the opening act for a well-known artist. Breaking into show business took a lot of hard work.

Isabella had become quite the traveler. She and Luce were able to leave the vineyard in Davidia's capable hands for longer and longer periods of time. Stephen and Helen were always glad to see them when they visited the estate in England, and the Moody's visited Chateau des Bois often. The two couples had become close friends over the years. They liked the same things and found traveling together most enjoyable. Stephen, like Luce, was leaving more and more of the running of the estate to the next generation. Much to the amusement of his friend, George would be Lord Moody someday. Joseph teased him about it every time they were together.

Bella had made several trips to America without Luce, who was finding the long trip too tiring. Joseph and his wife were world travelers so it was easier for everyone if they arranged to drop by the chateau on their way to or from somewhere. Joseph had commissioned a large painting of the chateau for his mother and Luce, and it now hung in a place of honor in the ballroom.

They were looking forward to a visit from Yvette and Lucien. Yvette had become an interior designer after the children had left for college and was in great demand. The age limit for pilots was fast approaching, and Lucien was facing retirement. They wanted to talk to Bella and Luce about an idea they had for a business. Davidia was excited to show her mother and father everything she had accomplished since their last visit. She had brought the vineyard into the twentieth century. The majestic old wooden vats, sat in their place, next to beautiful new machines that made the process so much easier to clean and to operate. Production was up and sales had reached an all-time high. Their vineyard might be small, but it was an example of modern efficiency without losing the quality. Luce was so proud of her, he couldn't wait to tell her parents.

Bella's daughter and her husband didn't understand everything their daughter was explaining about the new equipment, but they could tell Davidia was excited and happy. Luce had insisted on joining the tour of the vineyards and caves. He loved showing off his granddaughter's improvements to the winery. After lunch, he agreed with Bella that perhaps he should lie down for a little while. The morning exercise had taken its toll. The others took a walk and inspected the gardens and a new greenhouse that Bella was having erected. Yvette had brought things for Davidia's apartment. The ladies were in the suit admiring the new additions when Lucian appeared at the door. His face was grey, and the tears were streaming down his cheeks. "Bella, it's Luce. He didn't make it to the bedroom. He is in trouble."

Isabella rushed past him, hoping he was wrong. Luce was half sitting, half lying in a chair. It looked as if he had felt weak and decided to sit a minute before going into the bedroom. Bella had worked in hospitals long enough to see that there was nothing that could be done for her beloved Luce. She knelt beside his chair and took his hand. He opened his eyes and attempted to smile. His lips formed the words, "Love you." His wonderful big heart had betrayed him, and he had taken his last breath. Bella stayed there holding his hand, unwilling to let go, until at last her son-in-law took her arm and helped her up. He led her to the couch and gave her a brandy. She sat there, trying to think of what must be done. The tears could wait, right now she needed to take care of Luce. "A doctor should be called, also the police. We must notify the children. Luce had written out his wishes. They are in his lockbox in his office. A priest should be called, also a mortician." Bella began to shiver.

"We will take care of all that mother. Thank God we were here. Lucien will go into town and send wires to everyone. A doctor is coming, and the police have been notified." Yvette wrapped her mother in a shawl. "You need something hot." She put her arms around Bella and held her tight. "Davidia please go and make your Nanna some hot tea."

The police had come and gone. The mortician had ordered a coffin, and while the priest had taken umbrage over the idea that Luce would be buried in the chateau graveyard, rather than at the church, that had been Luce's written instructions. Joseph and his wife were flying in from New York, Yvette, and Lucien were staying at the house to help, and the rest of the grandchildren were doing their best to arrive in time for the funeral. As long as Isabella had things to do, she was able to manage. It was when she had time to stop and think, that there was a problem. Now she would take care of everything that needed to be done. Later, there would be time to face the fact that she was alone once more. She would have the rest of her life to mourn.

Luce had been laid to rest, and the children had returned to their own lives. Bella was slowly adjusting to the fact that Luce was no longer there. There were times when she forgot that he was gone and would think of something she wanted to tell him or reach for him in her sleep. He had been such an integral part of her life. It didn't seem possible for life to go on without him, but it did.

Stephen and Helen Moody had suggested that she come to England for a visit. Perhaps a change of scenery would be helpful. She thanked them for their kind invitation, but she had a new project to supervise. While the little graveyard had not been ignored, it seemed a bit shabby. A contractor had been called, and plans were drawn up to make it a more welcoming, peaceful place. Keeping busy would help.

Fifty-Three

Chapter 53. An Old Friend and a New Four-Legged One.

Time seemed to drag by, yet it had been a year since Luce had passed. Davidia had brought home a puppy. He was all legs and big feet. He was supposed to be her daughter's dog, but he had quickly chosen his mistress. Bella couldn't make a move without him. He followed her around and insisted on sleeping beside her bed. If the antique bed hadn't been so high, he would have happily shared it with her. His antics made her laugh, and he would seek to comfort her when the loneliness overwhelmed her. The dog was her constant companion, and she welcomed his presence. Gradually she was adjusting to being alone.

Lady Helen Moody had fallen ill and passed away. Bella had spent time by her bedside and helped Stephen to care for her until the end. She had been buried in the churchyard next to

Maude. Stephen had taken to drink, much to his son's dismay. He understood that his dad was using alcohol to deaden the pain of his mother's death, but he didn't want to lose his father as well. He consulted Bella as to what should be done.

Isabella was familiar with the problem. She remembered her addiction to the painkillers after Joe's death. It had taken almost losing Yvette to shock her enough to make her stop. George called the family together to confront his father and convinced him to seek professional help. Being able to talk about the loss of Helen with Bella, knowing she understood his pain, aided in his recovery. You must have experienced a thing, to truly understand.

George Moody, his wife, and the children had been living at the estate for years, so Stephen had felt that he was no longer needed. After his mother's death, George made a concerted effort to consult his father about things. When Stephen realized his son's intentions were to include him, he appreciated it. He had been careful in the past to keep his opinion to himself so as not to interfere with his son's decisions. Now he would speak up if he thought his ideas could help. Once again, he felt viable.

From time to time, he would visit with Bella at the chateau. The two old friends would talk about the war years, about Joe, Luce, Maude, and Helen. Jim and Andrew too were gone. They were the only ones left who remembered these things. They weren't living in the past, just sharing memories. Two brave warriors fighting a battle against time, knowing that in the end, time would win.

Fifty-Four

Chapter 54. The News of the Day.

Isabella loved to walk out into her garden and down the tree lined path to the little graveyard. She had built a pergola with a bench and a small fountain. She would sit there for hours with a book, or just sit there in the sun, the dog, either sleeping at her feet, or chasing butterflies that drifted on the breeze. Sometimes she would doze off, while talking to Luce about the children or grandchildren. She would tell him how well the vineyard was doing, or what new and wonderful things his family was accomplishing in the business or art world. Maurice was married and had become the father of a beautiful baby boy. They had named him Lucien. Everyone called him Luce.

Davidia had a fiancé, a fellow vintner. He owned a vineyard not far from theirs with a larger piece of land, but Chateau des

Bois carried the reputation for excellence. The two vineyards would become one and carry the name of the chateau. Bella's grandson, Dean had drawn up the legal documents that would protect the land and the name of the champagne house, if at any time there should be a dispute as to who owned what. Her brother had insisted on it. Davidia thought he was being silly, and that it wasn't necessary. Dean had said, "Hopefully, it would never be needed, but better safe than sorry."

The other children seemed to be so busy pursuing their careers, that they didn't have time for serious relationships. Josephine's name was linked from time to time with some celebrity, but nothing came of it. According to the magazines, Maria too, seemed to fall in and out of love at the drop of a hat. Her brother had become a well-known pianist, with requests for appearances all over Europe.

Isabella loved all of her grandchildren, but it was Davidia that lived at Chateau des Bois and was her constant companion. When she married, she and her new husband would reside there. Their children would grow up in the chateau. They would be the guardians of Luce's family home and his beloved vineyards. She couldn't think of anyone better qualified.

Talking to Luce felt as natural now, as when he had been alive. When she had written her will, it was with Luce that she discussed ways of dividing her estate. What each of their children should receive, as well as the grandchildren. Chateau des Bois was a huge piece of the puzzle but Davidia must have it. Was the answer to divide fifty percent of the yearly profit from the champagne sales between the others? There would be equal trusts for any great grandchildren when they reached twenty-one, or earlier for their education. The children would receive equal shares of whatever monies she had at the time of her death.

Chapter 55. The World Without Isabella

She was the only one left. Stephan had fought a valiant battle but, death had won. He had kept his wonderful sense of humor till the end. A young man had accompanied him on his last visit. Stephen needed a wheelchair and help with feeding and personal care. He had laughed and said, "The golden years are beginning to rust." Isabella would miss her dear friend.

They had discussed the fact that they were having difficulty with the small things that had been so easy years ago. Climbing stairs, or climbing in and out of antique beds had become a daily chore. Throwing a ball for the dog, wasn't easy, and putting something away on a high shelf was impossible. These were things that could only be understood by people of a certain age. They had commiserated together, saying, "But we are still here!" Now, she was the last one standing.

Davidia had come to call her for supper. She and the dog walked slowly back to the house. He seemed to understand that his mistress was no longer capable of hurrying. He escorted her to the door before leaving to chase a pesky squirrel. He had never caught one, but there was always a first time. He didn't see Bella trip and fall. Davidia found her lying on the entryway floor. The farmer's son carried her to her bed, and a doctor was called.

Bella drifted in and out of consciousness. Days passed. The children and grandchildren had been called. The doctor came and went. She didn't seem to be in pain, she looked as if she was sleeping peacefully. A smile lit up her face from time to time. The dog refused to leave the side of the bed. They had tried shutting him out, but his howling was so loud and prolonged, he had been allowed back in. He refused to eat and left her side only long enough to take care of his needs.

The family took turns watching by her bedside. No one could imagine a world without Isabella. She was the one constant in all their lives. She had always been there, through war and peace, births and deaths, sharing their triumphs and their defeats. Not having her there to turn to, was inconceivable. They talked in whispered tones when what they wanted, was to scream at her to please wake up.

Isabella had opened her eyes. Her granddaughter had gone to make her a cup of tea and share the good news with the rest of the family. The dog nuzzled her hand, hoping his mistress would get up. He couldn't understand what was happening, but he could feel the anxiety that permeated the air. She ruffled his fur and told him it was all right, then she shut her eyes once more.

Fifty-Six

Epilogue

***

They were gathering, the ones she loved in this world,
and those from the next. It was time, and Isabella
was ready. The room was flooded with light. She
remembered the promise she had made so long ago, or was it
yesterday? "Celebrate my life by living your life well." Sophia
had instructed. "Do not hold me back with your prayers and
tears when it is time for me to go." She had tried to live up
to those words of wisdom, and to pass them on. "The energy
that is Bella, will never die. It will only change form." She had
told them. The light was growing even brighter. "What an
extraordinary adventure my life has been." She thought. "How
blessed I am… Oh! How beautiful the light is… It is calling… A

new amazing adventure awaits."

Fifty-Seven

Afterwards. A New Book. "Bridget" From Rags to Riches.

⁕

Chapter 1 Too Many Questions.

The priest and the midwife were in the house with her mother. There was to be another baby. " A gift from God" according to the church. "If it was a gift, why did God keep sending them and then taking them back? Maybe He could send food instead" She had asked a nun this and the only answer was a hard blow to the ear. She soon learned not to ask these things. That didn't mean she didn't think them. All kinds of questions were running around in her head. " If the babies must be christened when they were born so that if they died, their souls would go to heaven, what about the babies that were born dead? Did they go to Hell? That didn't seem right. What sins had they committed?" Asking for an answer to that question would have gotten her a whipping from Mother

Superior.

Her brother and sisters were hungry and needed to be fed, but they had to wait until after the baby was born. The house consisted of one room, and that room was occupied. The little ones were beginning to cry. Her brother Patrick kicked the dirt and acted as if he didn't care if he ate. Earlier she had gone to the fields to find dandelion leaves. They could be eaten raw or cooked. The younger children didn't like them, but you ate what was available.

Her grandfather had shown her how to snare a rabbit. It could last for several days as a stew. She had been unable to leave the house, so now the larder was bare. Bridget had tried to show her brother how to catch one, but his coughing scared the rabbits off. There was blood on Patrick's snotty rag. That was not a good sign. Her beloved grandfather had died soon after he had begun to cough up blood.

The priest came from the house followed by the midwife carrying a small bundle. The baby had been born dead. She couldn't say she was sorry about that. They couldn't feed the children they had. Both the priest and the midwife would want payments for their labor. The purse was as empty as the larder.